Artrly

THE STRANGE CASE OF DR. JEKYLL AND MR. HYDE

Robert Louis Stevenson

*Supplementary material written by
Anna Maria Hong*

Series edited by Cynthia Brantley Johnson

SIMON & SCHUSTER PAPERBACKS
NEW YORK LONDON TORONTO SYDNEY

Simon & Schuster Paperbacks
A Division of Simon & Schuster, Inc.
1230 Avenue of the Americas
New York, NY 10020

This book is a work of fiction. Names, characters, places, and incidents either are products of the author's imagination or are used fictitiously. Any resemblance to actual events or locales or persons, living or dead, is entirely coincidental.

Supplementary materials copyright © 2005 by Simon & Schuster, Inc.

This Simon & Schuster paperback edition February 2011

SIMON & SCHUSTER PAPERBACKS and colophon are registered trademarks of Simon & Schuster, Inc.

For information regarding special discounts for bulk purchases, please contact Simon & Schuster Special Sales at 1-866-506-1949 or business@simonandschuster.com.

The Simon & Schuster Speakers Bureau can bring authors to your live event. For more information or to book an event, contact the Simon & Schuster Speakers Bureau at 1-866-248-3049 or visit our website at www.simonspeakers.com.

Cover illustration by Dan Craig

Manufactured in the United States of America

14   13   12   11   10   9   8   7   6   5

ISBN 978-1-4165-0021-6

To
Katharine de Mattos

It's ill to loose the bands that God decreed to bind;
Still will we be the children of the heather
   and the wind;
Far away from home, O it's still for you and me
That the broom is blowing bonnie in the
   north countrie.

Contents

THE STRANGE CASE OF DR. JEKYLL AND MR. HYDE

INTRODUCTION

The Strange Case of Dr. Jekyll and Mr. Hyde: A LITERARY "SHILLING SHOCKER"

Since its publication in 1886, *The Strange Case of Dr. Jekyll and Mr. Hyde* has remained continuously in print and has been translated over eighty times and into more than thirty languages. Always popular with ordinary readers, *Dr. Jekyll and Mr. Hyde* has also been admired by well-known writers as diverse as Henry James, Vladimir Nabokov, Joyce Carol Oates, Gerard Manley Hopkins, Jorge Luis Borges, and Italo Calvino. Many of these writers have noted that the source of the book's enduring appeal is a fast-paced plot combined with a masterful style. Robert Louis Stevenson was an erudite writer who had read voraciously since boyhood, but he wore his education lightly and was determined to write novels that would engage and entertain a wide audience. He dubbed *Dr. Jekyll and Mr. Hyde* a "shilling shocker," placing it alongside the many cheaply printed horror stories of the day known in England as "penny dreadfuls." But Stevenson's shocker has come to take its place alongside some of the most artistic of literary works.

Dr. Jekyll and Mr. Hyde propels the reader rapidly through an increasingly horrifying and fantastic tale to an ending that leaves the reader to contemplate the story's moral ambiguities. The novel focuses on the two-sided quality of human nature and society, exploring the tensions between good and evil, public and private, sensual and spiritual, self-control and freedom. It also offers a glimpse into the mores of Victorian society and its anxieties regarding the pitfalls of technological progress and social hypocrisy.

The novel's spare urgency may be partly attributable to the speed with which it was written. As reported in his 1888 essay "A Chapter on Dreams," the book's main events came to Stevenson in a dream. Employing these events to create his work on "man's double being," Stevenson wrote the first draft of the novel in three days. Though he burned that draft at his wife's suggestion, he wrote the final version in another three-day heat.

The book's main conceit—the title character's transformation from the respectable Dr. Jekyll to the unfettered Mr. Hyde—has endured as a metaphor for a modern psychological condition. The book has been adapted into numerous children's, stage, and film versions, including a 1931 classic starring Frederic March and humorous adaptations starring Abbott and Costello and Jerry Lewis. Prominent writers such as Susan Sontag have written versions of the tale, and Stevenson's brilliant story has popped up in popular cartoons including *The Mighty Mouse Playhouse* and *The Bugs Bunny Show*.

A blend of many genres including Gothic horror, science fiction, and romance, *Dr. Jekyll and Mr. Hyde* remains a riveting novel that leaves readers with a sense of unease as they recognize parts of themselves in both Jekyll and Hyde.

The Life and Work of Robert Louis Stevenson

Robert Louis Stevenson was born on November 13, 1850, in Edinburgh, Scotland. The only child of Thomas Stevenson, a successful civil engineer, and Margaret Isabella Balfour, Stevenson suffered from debilitating illnesses throughout his life. Although his frail health made schooling difficult, he was an avid reader. At seventeen he entered Edinburgh University to study lighthouse engineering, but soon made a compromise with his father and switched to law.

As a university student, Stevenson rebelled against his strict, Calvinist upbringing and played the bohemian. He began experimenting with writing styles and published his first work, *The Pentland Rising*. In 1873, he met Sidney Colvin, an English art scholar, who would become his mentor and friend, and Fanny Sitwell, his unrequited love and later friend. The same year, Stevenson traveled to the French Riviera in order to recover from severe respiratory illness, probably tuberculosis. While traveling to convalesce, Stevenson devoted himself to writing. His two travel books, *An Inland Voyage* (1878) and *Travels with a Donkey in the Cévennes* (1879), and many essays of this period established his reputation as a writer.

In 1876, Stevenson met and fell in love with Fanny Osbourne, an American woman in the midst of a divorce from her husband. To the dismay of his parents, Stevenson traveled to California to join her in 1879.

Sick and poor, Stevenson nearly died from ill health, but rallied and married Osbourne in 1880. With encouragement from his father, Stevenson took his new bride and her son to Scotland to reconnect with his family.

Seeking health, the Stevensons traveled to Davos, Switzerland, the Scottish Highlands, and the south of France during the early 1880s. Stevenson began writing *Treasure Island* with his stepson in 1881 and published his first collection of essays, *Virginibus Puerisque*, that year. From 1884 to 1887, the family lived in Bournemouth, England, where Stevenson met and befriended the American novelist Henry James. While at Bournemouth, he also wrote *Kidnapped*, *Dr. Jekyll and Mr. Hyde*, and "Markheim." He published *Prince Otto* and *A Child's Garden of Verses* in 1885. The publication of *Dr. Jekyll and Mr. Hyde* in 1886 propelled him to popular and literary fame. Finding the climate in Bournemouth bad for his health, Stevenson, along with his wife, stepson, and mother, went to the Adirondacks in upstate New York in 1887. Saranac Lake, in the Adirondacks, was the site of a famous tubercular sanitorium.

In 1888, the family sailed through the South Seas, visiting the Marquesas Islands, Fakarava Atoll, Tahiti, Honolulu, the Gilbert Islands, and finally Samoa. His writings on these travels include *In the South Seas* (1896) and *A Footnote to History* (1892). After a trip to Sydney, Australia, in 1890, Stevenson returned to Samoa and set up residence at a house called Vailima, where he spent the rest of his life. At Vailima he wrote *Island Nights' Entertainments* (1893) and *David Balfour* (1893), the sequel to *Kidnapped*, as well as *The*

Ebb-Tide (1894) (originated by Lloyd Osbourne). He also began his unfinished masterpiece, *Weir of Hermiston*, which was published posthumously in 1896. Stevenson died suddenly of a cerebral hemorrhage in 1894 and was buried, according to his wishes, on Mt. Vaea in Samoa.

In addition to writing novels, Stevenson wrote poems, essays, and copious letters. Popular and successful during his time, Stevenson's literary reputation suffered a decline soon after his death. However, by the 1950s critics again received Stevenson's works warmly, recognizing his novels as fast-paced and gripping stories with original and ambiguous moral themes.

Historical and Literary Context of *The Strange Case of Dr. Jekyll and Mr. Hyde*

The Victorian Era

Robert Louis Stevenson lived in the shadow of one of the most important figures of British history: Queen Victoria. The indomitable monarch had been ruling for thirteen years when he was born, and she outlived the sickly writer by seven years. During Victoria's reign, England underwent a startling and dramatic transformation from an influential agricultural society with a few overseas territories to an international, industrial superpower with control over vast swaths of land on almost every continent. By the end of the nineteenth century, it was a common, and accurate, English boast that "the sun never sets on the British Empire."

At the time of the publication of *The Strange Case of Dr. Jekyll and Mr. Hyde,* England had become an industrialized nation. Technological innovations had shifted the basis of England's economy from agriculture to industry between 1750 and 1850. The development of steam power and a boom in the cotton textiles industry caused a population shift from rural to urban areas. New steam-powered railroads and ships broadened the market for England's output. Laborers were more at the mercy of their employers than ever before, and working conditions in factories, mines, and mills were often brutal. Children and adults alike commonly worked as much as sixteen hours a day, six days a week, in dangerous conditions for very small wages. Throughout the nineteenth century, most of the Western world struggled to adjust to the impact of industrialization.

Enormous Change: Darwin, Marx, Freud

The Victorian age gave rise to scientific, social, and psychological theories that shook the foundations of accepted knowledge. The many breakthroughs in scientific, psychological, and social theory created doubt about the reliability of truth and humankind's role in the universe as it had been known. Charles Darwin's *On the Origin of Species* (1859) proposed a theory of evolution that challenged prevailing ideas of religious and social order. The full impact of *Origin of Species* took several decades to emerge, and we still feel it today. Karl Marx's radical economic theories outlining the perpetual class struggle between property-owning oppressors and exploited workers spurred the growth of socialism, called for an overthrow of the capitalist system, and helped give rise to a labor movement. Sigmund Freud, the founder of modern psychology and psychoanalysis, changed the way people thought of themselves by proposing that normality and madness lie on a continuum and are not utterly opposed. Though Freud's theories were still being formulated at the time Stevenson was writing *Dr. Jekyll and Mr. Hyde,* the novel anticipated many of the ideas that would become crucial to Freud's theories.

Stevenson's Influences

Stevenson was an avid reader. As a young man, he read Charles Dickens and William Makepeace Thackeray, as well as the romantic works of Sir Walter Scott and the thrilling horror stories of Edgar Allan Poe and Nathaniel Hawthorne. *Dr. Jekyll and Mr. Hyde* was influenced by these and other literary predecessors, especially Mary Shelley's Gothic novel *Frankenstein* (1818), in which a doctor's desires to create another using only technology results in disaster. The theme of the "double," so central to *Dr. Jekyll and Mr. Hyde,* makes many previous appearances in romantic and post-romantic literature, but is especially prominent in James Hogg's *The Private Memoirs and Confessions of a Justified Sinner* (1824). Hogg also makes use of multiple documents (such as letters and newspaper stories alongside of the traditional narrative) and viewpoints to give his novel a realistic feel. Shelley had used this technique in *Frankenstein,* and later, at the turn of the century, Bram Stoker used it in his 1897 horror classic, *Dracula.*

CHRONOLOGY OF ROBERT LOUIS STEVENSON'S LIFE AND WORK

1850: Robert Louis Stevenson born November 13 in Edinburgh, Scotland. The only child of prominent engineer Thomas Stevenson and Margaret Isabella Balfour, Stevenson grows up in Edinburgh suffering frequent debilitating illnesses.

1867: Enrolls at Edinburgh University to study engineering. Later switches to law and pursues interest in literature.

1873: Meets mentor-friend Sidney Colvin and confidante Frances Sitwell. Suffering from nervous exhaustion and illness, Stevenson winters in the south of France.

1875: Admitted to the Scottish Bar but soon abandons law to pursue writing.

1878: Publishes first books, *An Inland Voyage* and *Edinburgh: Picturesque Notes*.

1879: Travels to New York and California to be with future wife, Fanny Osbourne. Publishes *Travels with a Donkey in the Cévennes*.

1880: Nearly dies from lung hemorrhage. Marries Osbourne and returns to Scotland. Spends time in Davos, Switzerland, for health reasons.

1882–83: Publishes *Treasure Island* in serialized form, *Familiar Studies of Men and Books*, and *New Arabian Nights*. Relocates to south of France for health. Publishes *The Silverado Squatters*.

1884: Moves to Bournemouth, on south coast of England. Writes "Markheim" and several plays.

1885: Publishes *A Child's Garden of Verses* and *More New Arabian Nights: The Dynamiter*. Moves into "Skerryvore," a house bequeathed by Stevenson's father. Publishes *Prince Otto*. Has dream that leads to writing of *The Strange Case of Dr. Jekyll and Mr. Hyde*.

1886: Publishes *The Strange Case of Dr. Jekyll and Mr. Hyde* and *Kidnapped*.

1887: Moves to Saranac Lake, New York. Publishes *The Merry Men and Other Tales*, *Underwoods*, and *Memories and Portraits*.

1888: Writes essays for *Scribner's Magazine*. Takes cruise in the South Seas for health. Stops in Tahiti to convalesce.

1889: Ends cruise in Honolulu. Publishes *The Master of Ballantrae* and coauthors *The Wrong Box* with his stepson. Takes another cruise, ending in Samoa.

1890: Buys estate called "Vailima" on the island of Upolu, in Samoa.

1891: Moves permanently into Vailima and is given Samoan name of "Tusitala" (teller of tales). Publishes letters of voyages in serial form.

1892: Publishes *The Wrecker* and *A Footnote to History: Eight Years of Trouble in Samoa.*

1893: Publishes *David Balfour* and *Island Nights' Entertainments.*

1894: Publishes the *The Ebb-Tide.* Dies of cerebral hemorrhage and is buried at the top of Mt. Vaea, in Samoa.

1895: Posthumous publication of fables in *Longman's Magazine.*

1896: Posthumous publication of *Weir of Hermiston: An Unfinished Romance* and serial publication of *St. Ives.*

HISTORICAL CONTEXT OF
The Strange Case of Dr. Jekyll and Mr. Hyde

1837: Queen Victoria ascends to the throne of Great Britain.

1844: The First Factory Act is passed, limiting working hours in England.

1845: "The Great Hunger" or potato famine begins, killing millions in Ireland.

1848: Karl Marx publishes *The Communist Manifesto.*

1854: The Crimean War begins.

1856: End of the Crimean War.

1858: Cathode rays are discovered by German physicist Julius Plücker.

1859: Charles Darwin publishes *On the Origin of Species.*

1861: Prince Albert, the consort to Queen Victoria, dies.

1867: British vote extended to working-class males. First volume of Marx's *Das Kapital,* written with Friedrich Engels, is published.

1868: The modern typewriter is patented.

1876: Queen Victoria becomes empress of India. Alexander Graham Bell patents the invention of the telephone.

1879: Thomas Edison invents the incandescent lamp.

1880: First Boer War begins, ending in 1881.

1882: Robert Koch discovers and identifies the bacillus causing tuberculosis.

1883: First skyscraper is built in Chicago.

1887: Queen Victoria's Golden Jubilee.

1889: The Eiffel Tower is built in Paris, France.

1890: William James publishes *The Principles of Psychology*.

1895: The Lumière brothers develop the Cinematograph in France. German physics professor Wilhelm Conrad Roentgen discovers X-rays.

1897: Queen Victoria's Diamond Jubilee. Joseph Thomson discovers particles smaller than atoms.

1899: Second Boer War begins, lasting until 1902.

1900: Sigmund Freud publishes *The Interpretation of Dreams*.

1901: Queen Victoria dies.

THE STRANGE CASE OF
DR. JEKYLL AND MR. HYDE

Story of the Door

Mr. Utterson the lawyer was a man of a rugged countenance, that was never lighted by a smile; cold, scanty and embarrassed in discourse; backward in sentiment; lean, long, dusty, dreary, and yet somehow lovable. At friendly meetings, and when the wine was to his taste, something eminently human beaconed from his eye; something indeed which never found its way into his talk, but which spoke not only in these silent symbols of the after-dinner face, but more often and loudly in the acts of his life. He was austere with himself; drank gin when he was alone, to mortify a taste for vintages; and though he enjoyed the theatre, had not crossed the doors of one for twenty years. But he had an approved tolerance for others; sometimes wondering, almost with envy, at the high pressure of spirits involved in their misdeeds; and in any extremity inclined to help rather than to reprove. "I incline to Cain's heresy,"[1] he used to say quaintly: "I let my brother go to the devil in his own way." In this character it was frequently his fortune to be the last reputable acquaintance and the last good influence in the lives of down-going men. And to such as these, so long as they came about his chambers, he never marked a shade of change in his demeanour.

No doubt the feat was easy to Mr. Utterson; for he was undemonstrative at the best, and even his friendships seemed to be founded in a similar catholicity of good-nature. It is the mark of a modest man to accept his friendly circle ready made from the hands of opportunity; and that was the lawyer's way. His friends were those of his own blood, or those whom he had known the longest; his affections, like ivy, were the growth of time, they implied no aptness in the object. Hence, no doubt, the bond that united him to Mr. Richard Enfield, his distant kinsman, the well-known man about town. It was a nut to crack for many, what these two could see in each other, or what subject they could find in common. It was reported by those who encountered them in their Sunday walks, that they said nothing, looked singularly dull, and would hail with obvious relief the appearance of a friend. For all that, the two men put the greatest store by these excursions, counted them the chief jewel of each week, and not only set aside occasions of pleasure, but even resisted the calls of business, that they might enjoy them uninterrupted.

It chanced on one of these rambles that their way led them down a by street in a busy quarter of London. The street was small and what is called quiet, but it drove a thriving trade on the week-days. The inhabitants were all doing well, it seemed, and all emulously hoping to do better still, and laying out the surplus of their gains in coquetry; so that the shop fronts stood along that thoroughfare with an air of invitation, like rows of smiling saleswomen. Even on Sunday, when it veiled its more florid charms and lay comparatively empty of passage, the street shone out in contrast to its dingy neighbourhood, like a fire in a forest; and with its freshly painted shutters, well-polished brasses, and general cleanliness and gaiety of note, instantly caught and pleased the eye of the passenger.

Two doors from one corner, on the left hand going east, the line was broken by the entry of a court; and just at that point, a certain sinister block of building thrust forward its gable on the street. It was two storeys high; showed no window, nothing but a door on the lower storey and a blind forehead of discoloured wall on the upper; and bore in every feature the marks of prolonged and sordid negligence. The door, which was equipped with neither bell nor knocker, was blistered and distained.[2] Tramps slouched into the recess and struck matches on the panels; children kept shop upon the steps; the schoolboy had tried his knife on the mouldings; and for close on a generation no one had appeared to drive away these random visitors or to repair their ravages.

Mr. Enfield and the lawyer were on the other side of the by street; but when they came abreast of the entry, the former lifted up his cane and pointed.

"Did you ever remark that door?" he asked; and when his companion had replied in the affirmative, "It is connected in my mind," added he, "with a very odd story."

"Indeed!" said Mr. Utterson, with a slight change of voice, "and what was that?"

"Well, it was this way," returned Mr. Enfield: "I was coming home from some place at the end of the world, about three o'clock of a black winter morning, and my way lay through a part of town where there was literally nothing to be seen but lamps. Street after street, and all the folks asleep—street after street, all lighted up as if for a procession, and all as empty as a church—till at last I got into that state of mind when a man listens and listens and begins to long for the sight of a policeman. All at once, I saw two figures: one a little man who was stumping along eastward at a good walk, and the other a girl of maybe eight or ten who was running as hard as she was able down a cross-street. Well, sir, the two ran into one another naturally enough at the corner; and then came the horrible part of the thing; for the man trampled calmly over the child's body and left her screaming on the ground. It sounds nothing to hear, but it was hellish to see. It wasn't like a man; it was like some damned Juggernaut.[3] I gave a view halloa,[4] took to my heels, collared my gentleman, and brought him back to where there was already quite a group about the screaming child. He was perfectly cool and made no resistance, but gave me one look, so ugly that it brought out the sweat on me like running. The people who had turned out were the girl's own family; and pretty soon the doctor, for whom she had been sent, put in his appearance. Well, the child was not much the worse, more frightened, according to the Sawbones;[5] and there you might have supposed would be an end to it. But there was one curious circumstance. I had taken a loathing to my gentleman at first sight. So had the child's family, which was only natural. But the doctor's case was what struck me. He was the usual cut-and-dry apothecary, of no particular age and colour, with a strong Edinburgh accent, and about as emotional as a bagpipe. Well, sir,

he was like the rest of us: every time he looked at my
prisoner, I saw that Sawbones turned sick and white
with the desire to kill him. I knew what was in his mind,
just as he knew what was in mine; and killing being out
of the question, we did the next best. We told the man
we could and would make such a scandal out of this, as
should make his name stink from one end of London to
the other. If he had any friends or any credit, we under-
took that he should lose them. And all the time, as we
were pitching it in red hot, we were keeping the women
off him as best we could, for they were as wild as
harpies. I never saw a circle of such hateful faces; and
there was the man in the middle, with a kind of black
sneering coolness—frightened too, I could see that—
but carrying it off, sir, really like Satan. 'If you choose to
make capital out of this accident,' said he, 'I am naturally helpless. No gentleman but wishes to avoid a
scene,' says he. 'Name your figure.' Well, we screwed
him up to a hundred pounds for the child's family; he
would have clearly liked to stick out; but there was
something about the lot of us that meant mischief, and
at last he struck.[6] The next thing was to get the money;
and where do you think he carried us but to that place
with the door?—whipped out a key, went in, and
presently came back with the matter of ten pounds in
gold and a cheque for the balance on Coutts's,[7] drawn
payable to bearer, and signed with a name that I can't
mention, though it's one of the points of my story, but it
was a name at least very well known and often printed.
The figure was stiff; but the signature was good for
more than that, if it was only genuine. I took the liberty
of pointing out to my gentleman that the whole business looked apocryphal; and that a man does not, in re-

life, walk into a cellar door at four in the morning and come out of it with another man's cheque for close upon a hundred pounds. But he was quite easy and sneering. 'Set your mind at rest,' says he; 'I will stay with you till the banks open, and cash the cheque myself.' So we all set off, the doctor, and the child's father, and our friend and myself, and passed the rest of the night in my chambers; and next day, when we had breakfasted, went in a body to the bank. I gave in the cheque myself, and said I had every reason to believe it was a forgery. Not a bit of it. The cheque was genuine."

"Tut-tut!" said Mr. Utterson.

"I see you feel as I do," said Mr. Enfield. "Yes, it's a bad story. For my man was a fellow that nobody could have to do with, a really damnable man; and the person that drew the cheque is the very pink of the proprieties,[8] celebrated too, and (what makes it worse) one of your fellows who do what they call good. Blackmail, I suppose; an honest man paying through the nose for some of the capers of his youth. Blackmail House is what I call that place with the door, in consequence. Though even that, you know, is far from explaining all," he added; and with the words fell into a vein of musing.

From this he was recalled by Mr. Utterson asking rather suddenly: "And you don't know if the drawer of the cheque lives there?"

"A likely place, isn't it?" returned Mr. Enfield. "But I happen to have noticed his address; he lives in some square or other."

"And you never asked about—the place with the door?" said Mr. Utterson.

"No, sir: I had a delicacy," was the reply. "I feel very ⸱⸱gly about putting questions; it partakes too much of the style of the day of judgment. You start a question, and it's like starting a stone. You sit quietly on the top of a hill; and away the stone goes, starting others; and presently some bland old bird (the last you would have thought of) is knocked on the head in his own back garden, and the family have to change their name. No, sir, I make it a rule of mine: the more it looks like Queer Street,[9] the less I ask."

"A very good rule, too," said the lawyer.

"But I have studied the place for myself," continued Mr. Enfield. "It seems scarcely a house. There is no other door, and nobody goes in or out of that one, but, once in a great while, the gentleman of my adventure. There are three windows looking on the court on the first floor; none below; the windows are always shut, but they're clean. And then there is a chimney, which is generally smoking; so somebody must live there. And yet it's not so sure; for the buildings are so packed together about that court, that it's hard to say where one ends and another begins."

The pair walked on again for a while in silence; and then—"Enfield," said Mr. Utterson, "that's a good rule of yours."

"Yes, I think it is," returned Enfield.

"But for all that," continued the lawyer, "there's one point I want to ask: I want to ask the name of that man who walked over the child."

"Well," said Mr. Enfield, "I can't see what harm it would do. It was a man of the name of Hyde."

"Hm," said Mr. Utterson. "What sort of a man is he to see?"

"He is not easy to describe. There is something wrong with his appearance; something displeasing, something downright detestable. I never saw a man I so disliked, and yet I scarce know why. He must be deformed somewhere; he gives a strong feeling of deformity, although I couldn't specify the point. He's an extraordinary-looking man, and yet I really can name nothing out of the way. No, sir; I can make no hand of it; I can't describe him. And it's not want of memory; for I declare I can see him this moment."

Mr. Utterson again walked some way in silence, and obviously under a weight of consideration. "You are sure he used a key?" he inquired at last.

"My dear sir . . ." began Enfield, surprised out of himself.

"Yes, I know," said Utterson; "I know it must seem strange. The fact is, if I do not ask you the name of the other party, it is because I know it already. You see, Richard, your tale has gone home. If you have been inexact in any point, you had better correct it."

"I think you might have warned me," returned the other, with a touch of sullenness. "But I have been pedantically exact, as you call it. The fellow had a key; and, what's more, he has it still. I saw him use it, not a week ago."

Mr. Utterson sighed deeply, but said never a word; and the young man presently resumed. "Here is another lesson to say nothing," said he. "I am ashamed of my long tongue. Let us make a bargain never to refer to this again."

"With all my heart," said the lawyer. "I shake hands on that, Richard."

SEARCH FOR MR. HYDE

That evening Mr. Utterson came home to his bache-lor house in sombre spirits, and sat down to dinner without relish. It was his custom of a Sunday, when this meal was over, to sit close by the fire, a volume of some dry divinity on his reading-desk, until the clock of the neighbouring church rang out the hour of twelve, when he would go soberly and gratefully to bed. On this night, however, as soon as the cloth was taken away, he took up a candle and went into his business room. There he opened his safe, took from the most private part of it a document endorsed on the envelope as Dr. Jekyll's Will, and sat down with a clouded brow to study its contents. The will was holograph; for Mr. Utterson, though he took charge of it now that it was made, had refused to lend the least assistance in the making of it; it provided not only that, in case of the decease of Henry Jekyll, M.D., D.C.L., LL.D., F.R.S.,[1] &c., all his possessions were to pass into the hands of his "friend and benefac-tor Edward Hyde"; but that in case of Dr. Jekyll's "disappearance or unexplained absence for any period exceeding three calendar months," the said Edward Hyde should step into the said Henry Jekyll's shoes without further delay, and free from any burthen or obligation, beyond the payment of a few small sums to the members of the doctor's household. This document had long been the lawyer's eyesore. It offended him both as a lawyer and as a lover of the sane and customary sides of life, to whom the fanciful was the immodest. And hitherto it was his ignorance of Mr. Hyde that had swelled his indignation; now, by a sudden turn, it was his knowledge. It was already bad enough when the name was but a name of which he could learn no more. It was worse when it began to be clothed upon with detestable attributes; and out of the shifting, insubstantial mists that had so long baffled his eye, there leaped up the sudden, definite presentment of a fiend.

"I thought it was madness," he said, as he replaced the obnoxious paper in the safe; "and now I begin to fear it is disgrace."

With that he blew out his candle, put on a great coat, and set forth in the direction of Cavendish Square, that citadel of medicine, where his friend, the great Dr. Lanyon, had his house and received his crowding patients. "If any one knows, it will be Lanyon," he had thought.

The solemn butler knew and welcomed him; he was subjected to no stage of delay, but ushered direct from the door to the dining room, where Dr. Lanyon sat alone over his wine. This was a hearty, healthy, dapper, red-faced gentleman, with a shock of hair prematurely white, and a boisterous and decided manner. At sight of Mr. Utterson, he sprang up from his chair and welcomed him with both hands. The geniality, as was the way of the man, was somewhat theatrical to the eye; but it reposed on genuine feeling. For these two were old friends, old mates both at school and college, both thorough respecters of themselves and of each other, and, what does not always follow, men who thoroughly enjoyed each other's company.

After a little rambling talk, the lawyer led up to the subject which so disagreeably preoccupied his mind.

"I suppose, Lanyon," he said, "you and I must be the two oldest friends that Henry Jekyll has?"

"I wish the friends were younger," chuckled Dr. Lanyon. "But I suppose we are. And what of that? I see little of him now."

"Indeed!" said Utterson. "I thought you had a bond of common interest."

"We had," was his reply. "But it is more than ten years since Henry Jekyll became too fanciful for me. He began to go wrong, wrong in mind; and though, of course, I continue to take an interest in him for old sake's sake as they say, I see and I have seen devilish little of the man. Such unscientific balderdash," added the doctor, flushing suddenly purple, "would have estranged Damon and Pythias."[2]

This little spirt of temper was somewhat of a relief to Mr. Utterson. "They have only differed on some point of science," he thought; and being a man of no scientific passions (except in the matter of conveyancing),[3] he even added: "It is nothing worse than that!" He gave his friend a few seconds to recover his composure, and then approached the question he had come to put.

"Did you ever come across a *protégé* of his—one Hyde?" he asked.

"Hyde?" repeated Lanyon. "No. Never heard of him. Since my time."

That was the amount of information that the lawyer carried back with him to the great, dark bed on which he tossed to and fro until the small hours of the morning began to grow large. It was a night of little ease to his toiling mind, toiling in mere[4] darkness and besieged by questions.

Six o'clock struck on the bells of the church that was so conveniently near to Mr. Utterson's dwelling, and still he was digging at the problem. Hitherto it had touched him on the intellectual side alone; but now his imagination also was engaged, or rather enslaved; and as he lay and tossed in the gross darkness of the night and the curtained room, Mr. Enfield's tale went by before his mind in a scroll of lighted pictures. He would be aware of the great field of lamps of a nocturnal city; then of the figure of a man walking swiftly; then of a child running from the doctor's; and then these met, and that human Juggernaut trod the child down and passed on regardless of her screams. Or else he would see a room in a rich house, where his friend lay asleep, dreaming and smiling at his dreams; and then the door of that room would be opened, the curtains of the bed plucked apart, the sleeper recalled, and, lo! there would stand by his side a figure to whom power was given, and even at that dead hour he must rise and do its bidding.[5] The figure in these two phases haunted the lawyer all night; and if at any time he dozed over, it was but to see it glide more stealthily through sleeping houses, or move the more swiftly, and still the more swiftly, even to dizziness, through wider labyrinths of lamp-lighted city, and at every street corner crush a child and leave her screaming. And still the figure had no face by which he might know it; even in his dreams it had no face, or one that baffled him and melted before his eyes; and thus it was that there sprang up and grew apace in the lawyer's mind a singularly strong, almost an inordinate, curiosity to behold the features of the real Mr. Hyde. If he could but once set eyes on him, he thought the mystery would lighten and perhaps roll altogether away, as was the habit of mysterious things when well examined. He might see a reason for his friend's strange preference or bondage (call it which you please), and even for the startling clauses of the will. And at least it would be a face worth seeing: the face of a man who was without bowels of mercy: a face which had but to show itself to raise up, in the mind of the unimpressionable Enfield, a spirit of enduring hatred.

From that time forward, Mr. Utterson began to haunt the door in the by street of shops. In the morning before office hours, at noon when business was plenty and time scarce, at night under the face of the fogged city moon, by all lights and at all hours of solitude or concourse, the lawyer was to be found on his chosen post.

"If he be Mr. Hyde," he had thought, "I shall be Mr. Seek."

And at last his patience was rewarded. It was a fine dry night; frost in the air; the streets as clean as a ballroom floor; the lamps, unshaken by any wind, drawing a regular pattern of light and shadow. By ten o'clock, when the shops were closed, the by street was very solitary, and, in spite of the low growl of London from all around, very silent. Small sounds carried far; domestic sounds out of the houses were clearly audible on either side of the roadway; and the rumour of the approach of any passenger preceded him by a long time. Mr. Utterson had been some minutes at his post when he was aware of an odd light footstep drawing near. In the course of his nightly patrols he had long grown accustomed to the quaint effect with which the footfalls of a single person, while he is still a great way off, suddenly spring out distinct from the vast hum and clatter of the city. Yet his attention had never before been so sharply and decisively arrested: and it was with a strong, superstitious prevision of success that he withdrew into the entry of the court.

The steps drew swiftly nearer, and swelled out suddenly louder as they turned the end of the street. The lawyer, looking forth from the entry, could soon see what manner of man he had to deal with. He was small, and very plainly dressed; and the look of him, even at that distance, went somehow strongly against the watcher's inclination. But he made straight for the door, crossing the roadway to save time; and as he came, he drew a key from his pocket, like one approaching home.

Mr. Utterson stepped out and touched him on the shoulder as he passed. "Mr. Hyde, I think?"

Mr. Hyde shrank back with a hissing intake of the breath. But his fear was only momentary; and though he did not look the lawyer in the face, he answered coolly enough: "That is my name. What do you want?"

"I see you are going in," returned the lawyer. "I am an old friend of Dr. Jekyll's—Mr. Utterson, of Gaunt Street—you must have heard my name; and meeting you so conveniently, I thought you might admit me."

"You will not find Dr. Jekyll; he is from home," replied Mr. Hyde, blowing in the key. And then suddenly, but still without looking up, "How did you know me?" he asked.

"On your side," said Mr. Utterson, "will you do me a favour?"

"With pleasure," replied the other. "What shall it be?"

"Will you let me see your face?" asked the lawyer.

Mr. Hyde appeared to hesitate; and then, as if upon some sudden reflection, fronted about with an air of defiance; and the pair stared at each other pretty fixedly for a few seconds. "Now I shall know you again," said Mr. Utterson. "It may be useful."

"Yes," returned Mr. Hyde, "it is as well we have met; and *à propos*, you should have my address." And he gave a number of a street in Soho.

"Good God!" thought Mr. Utterson, "can he too have been thinking of the will?" But he kept his feelings to himself, and only grunted in acknowledgment of the address.

"And now," said the other, "how did you know me?"

"By description," was the reply.

"Whose description?"

"We have common friends," said Mr. Utterson.

"Common friends!" echoed Mr. Hyde, a little hoarsely. "Who are they?"

"Jekyll, for instance," said the lawyer.

"He never told you," cried Mr. Hyde, with a flush of anger. "I did not think you would have lied."

"Come," said Mr. Utterson, "that is not fitting language."

The other snarled aloud into a savage laugh; and the next moment, with extraordinary quickness, he had unlocked the door and disappeared into the house.

The lawyer stood awhile when Mr. Hyde had left

him, the picture of disquietude. Then he began slowly
to mount the street, pausing every step or two, and
putting his hand to his brow like a man in mental per-
plexity. The problem he was thus debating as he walked
was one of a class that is rarely solved. Mr. Hyde was
pale and dwarfish; he gave an impression of deformity
without any namable malformation, he had a displeasing smile, he had borne himself to the lawyer with a sort
of murderous mixture of timidity and boldness, and he
spoke with a husky, whispering and somewhat broken
voice,—all these were points against him; but not all
of these together could explain the hitherto unknown
disgust, loathing and fear with which Mr. Utterson regarded him. "There must be something else," said the
perplexed gentleman. "There *is* something more, if I
could find a name for it. God bless me, the man seems
hardly human! Something troglodytic,[6] shall we say? or
can it be the old story of Dr. Fell?[7] or is it the mere radi-
ance of a foul soul that thus transpires through, and
transfigures, its clay continent?[8] The last, I think; for, O
my poor old Harry[9] Jekyll, if ever I read Satan's signature upon a face, it is on that of your new friend!"

Round the corner from the by street there was a
square of ancient, handsome houses, now for the most
part decayed from their high estate, and let in flats and
chambers to all sorts and conditions of men: map-
engravers, architects, shady lawyers, and the agents of
obscure enterprises. One house, however, second from
the corner, was still occupied entire; and at the door of
this, which wore a great air of wealth and comfort,
though it was now plunged in darkness except for the
fan-light, Mr. Utterson stopped and knocked. A well-
dressed, elderly servant opened the door.

"Is Dr. Jekyll at home, Poole?"[10] asked the lawyer.

"I will see, Mr. Utterson," said Poole, admitting the visitor, as he spoke, into a large, low-roofed, comfortable hall, paved with flags, warmed (after the fashion of a country house) by a bright, open fire, and furnished with costly cabinets of oak. "Will you wait here by the fire, sir? or shall I give you a light in the dining-room?"

"Here, thank you," said the lawyer; and he drew near and leaned on the tall fender. This hall, in which he was now left alone, was a pet fancy of his friend the doctor's; and Utterson himself was wont to speak of it as the pleasantest room in London. But to-night there was a shudder in his blood; the face of Hyde sat heavy on his memory; he felt (what was rare in him) a nausea and distaste of life; and in the gloom of his spirits, he seemed to read a menace in the flickering of the fire-light on the polished cabinets and the uneasy starting of the shadow on the roof. He was ashamed of his relief when Poole presently returned to announce that Dr. Jekyll was gone out.

"I saw Mr. Hyde go in by the old dissecting-room door, Poole," he said. "Is that right, when Dr. Jekyll is from home?"

"Quite right, Mr. Utterson, sir," replied the servant. "Mr. Hyde has a key."

"Your master seems to repose a great deal of trust in that young man, Poole," resumed the other, musingly.

"Yes, sir, he do indeed," said Poole. "We have all orders to obey him."

"I do not think I ever met Mr. Hyde?" asked Utterson.

"O dear no, sir. He never *dines* here," replied the butler. "Indeed, we see very little of him on this side of the house; he mostly comes and goes by the laboratory."

"Well, good-night, Poole."

"Good-night, Mr. Utterson."

And the lawyer set out homeward with a very heavy heart. "Poor Harry Jekyll," he thought, "my mind misgives me he is in deep waters! He was wild when he was young; a long while ago, to be sure; but in the law of God there is no statute of limitations. Ah, it must be that; the ghost of some old sin, the cancer of some concealed disgrace; punishment coming, *pede claudo*,[11] years after memory has forgotten and self-love condoned the fault." And the lawyer, scared by the thought, brooded awhile on his own past, groping in all the corners of memory, lest by chance some Jack-in-the-Box[12] of an old iniquity should leap to light there. His past was fairly blameless; few men could read the rolls of their life with less apprehension; yet he was humbled to the dust by the many ill things he had done, and raised up again into a sober and fearful gratitude by the many that he had come so near to doing, yet avoided. And then by a return on his former subject, he conceived a spark of hope. "This Master Hyde, if he were studied," thought he, "must have secrets of his own: black secrets, by the look of him; secrets compared to which poor Jekyll's worst would be like sunshine. Things cannot continue as they are. It turns me quite cold to think of this creature stealing like a thief to Harry's bedside; poor Harry, what a wakening! And the danger of it! for if this Hyde suspects the existence of the will, he may grow impatient to inherit. Ay, I must put my shoulder to the wheel—if Jekyll will but let me," he added, "if Jekyll will only let me." For once more he saw before his mind's eye, as clear as a transparency, the strange clauses of the will.

Dr. Jekyll Was Quite at Ease

A fortnight later, by excellent good fo
tor gave one of his pleasant dinners
six old cronies, all intelligent reputable
judges of good wine; and Mr. Utterson so
he remained behind after the others had
was no new arrangement, but a thing tha
many scores of times. Where Utterson was
liked well. Hosts loved to detain the dry
the light-hearted and the loose-tongued
their foot on the threshold; they liked to sit
unobtrusive company, practising for solitud
their minds in the man's rich silence, after
and strain of gaiety. To this rule Dr. Jekyll wa
tion; and as he now sat on the opposite side o
a large, well-made, smooth-faced man of
something of a slyish cast perhaps, but ever
capacity and kindness—you could see by his
he cherished for Mr. Utterson a sincere and warm
affection.

"I have been wanting to speak to you, Jekyll," began the latter. "You know that will of yours?"

A close observer might have gathered that the topic was distasteful; but the doctor carried it off gaily. "My poor Utterson," said he, "you are unfortunate in such a client. I never saw a man so distressed as you were by my will; unless it were that hide-bound pedant, Lanyon, at what he called my scientific heresies. O, I know he's a good fellow—you needn't frown—an excellent fellow, and I always mean to see more of him; but a hide-bound pedant for all that; an ignorant, blatant pedant. I was never more disappointed in any man than Lanyon."

"You know I never approved of it," pursued Utterson, ruthlessly disregarding the fresh topic.

"My will? Yes, certainly, I know that," said the doctor, a trifle sharply. "You have told me so."

"Well, I tell you so again," continued the lawyer. "I have been learning something of young Hyde."

The large handsome face of Dr. Jekyll grew pale to the very lips, and there came a blackness about his eyes. "I do not care to hear more," said he. "This is a matter I thought we had agreed to drop."

"What I heard was abominable," said Utterson.

"It can make no change. You do not understand my position," returned the doctor, with a certain incoherency of manner. "I am painfully situated, Utterson; my position is a very strange—a very strange one. It is one of those affairs that cannot be mended by talking."

"Jekyll," said Utterson, "you know me: I am a man to be trusted. Make a clean breast of this in confidence; and I make no doubt I can get you out of it."

"My good Utterson," said the doctor, "this is very good of you, this is downright good of you, and I cannot find words to thank you in. I believe you fully; I would trust you before any man alive, ay, before myself, if I could make the choice; but indeed it isn't what you fancy; it is not so bad as that; and just to put your good heart at rest, I will tell you one thing: the moment I choose, I can be rid of Mr. Hyde. I give you my hand upon that; and I thank you again and again; and I will just add one little word, Utterson, that I'm sure you'll take in good part: this is a private matter, and I beg of you to let it sleep."

Utterson reflected a little, looking in the fire.

"I have no doubt you are perfectly right," he said at last, getting to his feet.

"Well, but since we have touched upon this business, and for the last time, I hope," continued the doctor, "there is one point I should like you to understand. I have really a very great interest in poor Hyde. I know you have seen him; he told me so; and I fear he was rude. But I do sincerely take a great, a very great interest in that young man; and if I am taken away, Utterson, I wish you to promise me that you will bear with him and get his rights for him. I think you would, if you knew all; and it would be a weight off my mind if you would promise."

"I can't pretend that I shall ever like him," said the lawyer.

"I don't ask that," pleaded Jekyll, laying his hand upon the other's arm; "I only ask for justice; I only ask you to help him for my sake, when I am no longer here."

Utterson heaved an irrepressible sigh. "Well," said he, "I promise."

THE CAREW MURDER CASE

Nearly a year later, in the month of October, 18——, London was startled by a crime of singular ferocity, and rendered all the more notable by the high position of the victim. The details were few and startling. A maid-servant living alone in a house not far from the river had gone upstairs to bed about eleven. Although a fog rolled over the city in the small hours, the early part of the night was cloudless, and the lane, which the maid's window overlooked, was brilliantly lit by the full moon. It seems she was romantically given; for she sat down upon her box, which stood immediately under the window, and fell into a dream of musing. Never (she used to say, with streaming tears, when she narrated that experience), never had she felt more at peace with all men or thought more kindly of the world. And as she so sat she became aware of an aged and beautiful gentleman with white hair drawing near along the lane; and advancing to meet him, another and very small gentleman, to whom at first she paid less attention. When they had come within speech (which was just under the maid's eyes) the older man bowed and accosted the other with a very pretty manner of politeness. It did not seem as if the subject of his address were of great importance; indeed, from his pointing, it sometimes appeared as if he were only inquiring his way; but the moon shone on his face as he spoke, and the girl was pleased to watch it, it seemed to breathe such an innocent and old-world kindness of disposition, yet with something high too, as of a well-founded self-content. Presently her eye wandered to the other, and she was surprised to recognise in him a certain Mr. Hyde, who had once visited her master and for whom she had conceived a dislike. He had in his hand a heavy cane, with which he was trifling; but he answered never a word, and seemed to listen with an ill-contained impatience. And then all of a sudden he broke out in a great flame of anger, stamping with his foot, brandishing the cane, and carrying on (as the maid described it) like a madman. The old gentleman took a step back, with the air of one very much surprised and a trifle hurt; and at that Mr. Hyde broke out of all bounds, and clubbed him to the earth. And next moment, with ape-like fury, he was trampling his victim under foot, and hailing down a storm of blows, under which the bones were audibly shattered and the body jumped upon the roadway. At the horror of these sights and sounds, the maid fainted.

It was two o'clock when she came to herself and called for the police. The murderer was gone long ago; but there lay his victim in the middle of the lane, incredibly mangled. The stick with which the deed had been done, although it was of some rare and very tough and heavy wood, had broken in the middle under the stress of this insensate cruelty; and one splintered half had rolled in the neighbouring gutter—the other, without doubt, had been carried away by the murderer. A purse and a gold watch were found upon the victim; but no cards or papers, except a sealed and stamped envelope, which he had been probably carrying to the post, and which bore the name and address of Mr. Utterson.

This was brought to the lawyer the next morning, before he was out of bed; and he had no sooner seen it, and been told the circumstances, than he shot out a solemn lip. "I shall say nothing till I have seen the body," said he; "this may be very serious. Have the kindness to wait while I dress." And with the same grave countenance, he hurried through his breakfast and drove to the police station, whither the body had been carried. As soon as he came into the cell, he nodded.

"Yes," said he, "I recognise him. I am sorry to say that this is Sir Danvers Carew."

"Good God, sir!" exclaimed the officer, "is it possible?" And the next moment his eye lighted up with professional ambition. "This will make a deal of noise," he said. "And perhaps you can help us to the man." And he briefly narrated what the maid had seen, and showed the broken stick.

Mr. Utterson had already quailed at the name of Hyde; but when the stick was laid before him, he could doubt no longer: broken and battered as it was, he recognised it for one that he had himself presented many years before to Henry Jekyll.

"Is this Mr. Hyde a person of small stature?" he inquired.

"Particularly small and particularly wicked-looking, is what the maid calls him," said the officer.

Mr. Utterson reflected; and then, raising his head, "If you will come with me in my cab," he said, "I think I can take you to his house."

It was by this time about nine in the morning, and the first fog of the season. A great chocolate-coloured pall lowered over heaven, but the wind was continually charging and routing these embattled vapours; so that as the cab crawled from street to street, Mr. Utterson beheld a marvellous number of degrees and hues of twilight; for here it would be dark like the back-end of evening; and there would be a glow of a rich, lurid brown, like the light of some strange conflagration; and here, for a moment, the fog would be quite broken up, and a haggard shaft of daylight would glance in between the swirling wreaths. The dismal quarter of Soho seen under these changing glimpses, with its muddy ways, and slatternly passengers, and its lamps, which had never been extinguished or had been kindled afresh to combat this mournful reinvasion of darkness, seemed, in the lawyer's eyes, like a district of some city in a nightmare. The thoughts of his mind, besides, were of the gloomiest dye; and when he glanced at the companion of his drive, he was conscious of some touch of that terror of the law and the law's officers which may at times assail the most honest.

As the cab drew up before the address indicated, the fog lifted a little and showed him a dingy street, a gin palace,[1] a low French eating-house, a shop for the retail of penny numbers[2] and two-penny salads, many ragged children huddled in the doorways, and many women of many different nationalities passing out, key in hand, to have a morning glass; and the next moment the fog settled down again upon that part, as brown as umber, and cut him off from his blackguardly surroundings. This was the home of Henry Jekyll's favourite; of a man who was heir to a quarter of a million sterling.

An ivory-faced and silvery-haired old woman opened the door. She had an evil face, smoothed by hypocrisy; but her manners were excellent. Yes, she said, this was Mr. Hyde's, but he was not at home; he had been in that night very late, but had gone away again in less than an hour: there was nothing strange in that; his habits were very irregular, and he was often absent; for instance, it was nearly two months since she had seen him till yesterday.

"Very well then, we wish to see his rooms," said the lawyer; and when the woman began to declare it was impossible, "I had better tell you who this person is," he added. "This is Inspector Newcomen of Scotland Yard."

A flash of odious joy appeared upon the woman's face. "Ah!" said she, "he is in trouble! What has he done?"

Mr. Utterson and the inspector exchanged glances. "He don't seem a very popular character," observed the latter. "And now, my good woman, just let me and this gentleman have a look about us."

In the whole extent of the house, which but for the old woman remained otherwise empty, Mr. Hyde had only used a couple of rooms; but these were furnished with luxury and good taste. A closet was filled with wine; the plate was of silver, the napery elegant; a good picture hung upon the walls, a gift (as Utterson supposed) from Henry Jekyll, who was much of a connoisseur; and the carpets were of many plies and agreeable in colour. At this moment, however, the rooms bore every mark of having been recently and hurriedly ransacked; clothes lay about the floor, with their pockets inside out; lockfast drawers stood open; and on the hearth there lay a pile of grey ashes, as though many papers had been burned. From these embers the inspector disinterred the butt end of a green cheque book, which had resisted the action of the fire; the other half of the stick was found behind the door; and as this clinched his suspicions, the officer declared himself delighted. A visit to the bank, where several thousand pounds were found to be lying to the murderer's credit, completed his gratification.

"You may depend upon it, sir," he told Mr. Utterson. "I have him in my hand. He must have lost his head, or he never would have left the stick or, above all, burned the cheque book. Why, money's life to the man. We have nothing to do but wait for him at the bank, and get out the handbills."

This last, however, was not so easy of accomplishment; for Mr. Hyde had numbered few familiars—even the master of the servant-maid had only seen him twice; his family could nowhere be traced; he had never been photographed; and the few who could describe him differed widely, as common observers will. Only on one point were they agreed; and that was the haunting sense of unexpressed deformity with which the fugitive impressed his beholders.

Chapter 5

INCIDENT OF THE LETTER

It was late in the afternoon when Mr. Utterson found his way to Dr. Jekyll's door, where he was at once admitted by Poole, and carried down by the kitchen offices and across a yard which had once been a garden, to the building which was indifferently known as the laboratory or the dissecting-rooms. The doctor had bought the house from the heirs of a celebrated surgeon; and his own tastes being rather chemical than anatomical, had changed the destination of the block at the bottom of the garden. It was the first time that the lawyer had been received in that part of his friend's quarters; and he eyed the dingy windowless structure with curiosity, and gazed round with a distasteful sense of strangeness as he crossed the theatre,[1] once crowded with eager students and now lying gaunt and silent, the tables laden with chemical apparatus, the floor strewn with crates and littered with packing straw, and the light falling dimly through the foggy cupola. At the further end, a flight of stairs mounted to a door covered with red baize; and through this Mr. Utterson was at last received into the doctor's cabinet. It was a large room, fitted round with glass presses, furnished, among other things, with a cheval-glass[2] and a business table, and looking out upon the court by three dusty windows barred with iron. The fire burned in the grate; a lamp was set lighted on the chimney-shelf, for even in the houses the fog began to lie thickly; and there, close up to the warmth, sat Dr. Jekyll, looking deadly sick. He did not rise to meet his visitor, but held out a cold hand and bade him welcome in a changed voice.

"And now," said Mr. Utterson, as soon as Poole had left them, "you have heard the news?"

The doctor shuddered. "They were crying it in the square," he said. "I heard them in my dining room."

"One word," said the lawyer. "Carew was my client, but so are you; and I want to know what I am doing. You have not been mad enough to hide this fellow?"

"Utterson, I swear to God," cried the doctor, "I swear to God I will never set eyes on him again. I bind my honour to you that I am done with him in this world. It is all at an end. And indeed he does not want my help; you do not know him as I do; he is safe, he is quite safe; mark my words, he will never more be heard of."

The lawyer listened gloomily; he did not like his friend's feverish manner. "You seem pretty sure of him," said he; "and for your sake, I hope you may be right. If it came to a trial, your name might appear."

"I am quite sure of him," replied Jekyll; "I have grounds for certainty that I cannot share with any one. But there is one thing on which you may advise me. I have—I have received a letter; and I am at a loss whether I should show it to the police. I should like to leave it in your hands, Utterson; you would judge wisely, I am sure; I have so great a trust in you."

"You fear, I suppose, that it might lead to his detection?" asked the lawyer.

"No," said the other. "I cannot say that I care what becomes of Hyde; I am quite done with him. I was thinking of my own character, which this hateful business has rather exposed."

Utterson ruminated awhile; he was surprised at his friend's selfishness, and yet relieved by it. "Well," said he, at last, "let me see the letter."

The letter was written in an odd, upright hand, and signed "Edward Hyde": and it signified, briefly enough, that the writer's benefactor, Dr. Jekyll, whom he had long so unworthily repaid for a thousand generosities, need labour under no alarm for his safety as he had means of escape on which he placed a sure dependence. The lawyer liked this letter well enough; it put a better colour on the intimacy than he had looked for, and he blamed himself for some of his past suspicions.

"Have you the envelope?" he asked.

"I burned it," replied Jekyll, "before I thought what I was about. But it bore no postmark. The note was handed in."

"Shall I keep this and sleep upon it?" asked Utterson.

"I wish you to judge for me entirely," was the reply. "I have lost confidence in myself."

"Well, I shall consider," returned the lawyer. "And now one word more: it was Hyde who dictated the terms in your will about that disappearance?"

The doctor seemed seized with a qualm of faintness; he shut his mouth tight and nodded.

"I knew it," said Utterson. "He meant to murder you. You have had a fine escape."

"I have had what is far more to the purpose," returned the doctor solemnly: "I have had a lesson—O God, Utterson, what a lesson I have had!" And he covered his face for a moment with his hands.

On his way out, the lawyer stopped and had a word or two with Poole. "By the by," said he, "there was a letter handed in today: what was the messenger like?" But Poole was positive nothing had come except by post; "and only circulars by that," he added.

This news sent off the visitor with his fears renewed. Plainly the letter had come by the laboratory door; possibly, indeed, it had been written in the cabinet; and, if that were so, it must be differently judged, and handled with the more caution. The news boys, as he went, were crying themselves hoarse along the footways: "Special edition. Shocking murder of an M.P."[3] That was the funeral oration of one friend and client; and he could not help a certain apprehension lest the good name of another should be sucked down in the eddy of the scandal. It was, at least, a ticklish decision that he had to make; and, self-reliant as he was by habit, he began to cherish a longing for advice. It was not to be had directly; but perhaps, he thought, it might be fished for.

Presently after, he sat on one side of his own hearth, with Mr. Guest, his head clerk, upon the other, and midway between, at a nicely calculated distance from the fire, a bottle of a particular old wine that had long dwelt unsunned in the foundations of his house. The fog still slept on the wing above the drowned city, where the lamps glimmered like carbuncles; and through the muffle and smother of these fallen clouds, the procession of the town's life was still rolling in through the great arteries with a sound as of a mighty wind. But the room was gay with firelight. In the bottle the acids were long ago resolved; the imperial dye had softened with time, as the colour grows richer in stained windows; and the glow of hot autumn afternoons on hillside vineyards was ready to be set free and to disperse the fogs of London. Insensibly the lawyer melted. There was no man from whom he kept fewer secrets than Mr. Guest; and he was not always sure that he kept as many as he meant. Guest had often been on business to the doctor's; he knew Poole; he could scarce have failed to hear of Mr. Hyde's familiarity about the house; he might draw conclusions: was it not as well, then, that he should see a letter which put that mystery to rights? and above all, since Guest, being a great student and critic of handwriting, would consider the step natural and obliging? The clerk, besides, was a man of counsel; he would scarce read so strange a document without dropping a remark; and by that remark Mr. Utterson might shape his future course.

"This is a sad business about Sir Danvers," he said.

"Yes, sir, indeed. It has elicited a great deal of public feeling," returned Guest. "The man, of course, was mad."

"I should like to hear your views on that," replied Utterson. "I have a document here in his handwriting; it is between ourselves, for I scarce know what to do about it; it is an ugly business at the best. But there it is; quite in your way: a murderer's autograph."

Guest's eyes brightened, and he sat down at once and studied it with passion. "No, sir," he said; "not mad; but it is an odd hand."

"And by all accounts a very odd writer," added the lawyer.

Just then the servant entered with a note.

"Is that from Dr. Jekyll, sir?" inquired the clerk. "I thought I knew the writing. Anything private, Mr. Utterson?"

"Only an invitation to dinner. Why? Do you want to see it?"

"One moment. I thank you, sir"; and the clerk laid the two sheets of paper alongside and sedulously compared their contents. "Thank you, sir," he said at last, returning both; "it's a very interesting autograph."

There was a pause, during which Mr. Utterson struggled with himself. "Why did you compare them, Guest?" he inquired suddenly.

"Well, sir," returned the clerk, "there's a rathe singular resemblance; the two hands are in many points identical; only differently sloped."

"Rather quaint," said Utterson.

"It is, as you say, rather quaint," returned Guest.

"I wouldn't speak of this note, you know," said the master.

"No, sir," said the clerk. "I understand."

But no sooner was Mr. Utterson alone that night than he locked the note into his safe, where it reposed from that time forward. "What!" he thought. "Henry Jekyll forge for a murderer!" And his blood ran cold in his veins.

Remarkable Incident of Dr. Lanyon

Time ran on; thousands of pounds were offered in reward, for the death of Sir Danvers was resented as a public injury; but Mr. Hyde had disappeared out of the ken of the police as though he had never existed. Much of his past was unearthed, indeed, and all disreputable: tales came out of the man's cruelty, at once so callous and violent, of his vile life, of his strange associates, of the hatred that seemed to have surrounded his career; but of his present whereabouts, not a whisper. From the time he had left the house in Soho on the morning of the murder, he was simply blotted out; and gradually, as time drew on, Mr. Utterson began to recover from the hotness of his alarm, and to grow more at quiet with himself. The death of Sir Danvers was, to his way of thinking, more than paid for by the disappearance of Mr. Hyde. Now that that evil influence had been withdrawn, a new life began for Dr. Jekyll. He came out of his seclusion, renewed relations with his friends, became once more their familiar guest and entertainer; and whilst he had always been known for charities, he was now no less distinguished for religion. He was busy, he was much in the open air, he did good; his face seemed to open and brighten, as if with an inward consciousness of service; and for more than two months the doctor was at peace.

On the 8th of January Utterson had dined at the doctor's with a small party; Lanyon had been there; and the face of the host had looked from one to the other as in the old days when the trio were inseparable friends. On the 12th, and again on the 14th, the door was shut against the lawyer. "The doctor was confined to the house," Poole said, "and saw no one." On the 15th he tried again, and was again refused; and having now been used for the last two months to see his friend almost daily, he found this return of solitude to weigh upon his spirits. The fifth night he had in Guest to dine with him; and the sixth he betook himself to Dr. Lanyon's.

There at least he was not denied admittance; but when he came in, he was shocked at the change which had taken place in the doctor's appearance. He had his death-warrant written legibly upon his face. The rosy man had grown pale; his flesh had fallen away; he was visibly balder and older; and yet it was not so much these tokens of a swift physical decay that arrested the lawyer's notice, as a look in the eye and quality of manner that seemed to testify to some deep-seated terror of the mind. It was unlikely that the doctor should fear death; and yet that was what Utterson was tempted to suspect. "Yes," he thought; "he is a doctor, he must know his own state and that his days are counted; and the knowledge is more than he can bear." And yet when

Utterson remarked on his ill looks, it was with an air of great firmness that Lanyon declared himself a doomed man.

"I have had a shock," he said, "and I shall never recover. It is a question of weeks. Well, life has been pleasant; I liked it; yes, sir, I used to like it. I sometimes think if we knew all, we should be more glad to get away."

"Jekyll is ill, too," observed Utterson. "Have you seen him?"

But Lanyon's face changed, and he held up a trembling hand. "I wish to see or hear no more of Dr. Jekyll," he said, in a loud, unsteady voice. "I am quite done with that person; and I beg that you will spare me any allusion to one whom I regard as dead."

"Tut, tut," said Mr. Utterson; and then, after a considerable pause, "Can't I do anything?" he inquired. "We are three very old friends, Lanyon; we shall not live to make others."

"Nothing can be done," returned Lanyon; "ask himself."

"He will not see me," said the lawyer.

"I am not surprised at that," was the reply. "Some day, Utterson, after I am dead, you may perhaps come to learn the right and wrong of this. I cannot tell you. And in the meantime, if you can sit and talk with me of other things, for God's sake, stay and do so; but if you cannot keep clear of this accursed topic, then, in God's name, go, for I cannot bear it."

As soon as he got home, Utterson sat down and wrote to Jekyll, complaining of his exclusion from the house, and asking the cause of this unhappy break with

Lanyon; and the next day brought him a long answer, often very pathetically worded, and sometimes darkly mysterious in drift. The quarrel with Lanyon was incurable. "I do not blame our old friend," Jekyll wrote, "but I share his view that we must never meet. I mean from henceforth to lead a life of extreme seclusion; you must not be surprised, nor must you doubt my friendship, if my door is often shut even to you. You must suffer me to go my own dark way. I have brought on myself a punishment and a danger that I cannot name. If I am the chief of sinners, I am the chief of sufferers also. I could not think that this earth contained a place for sufferings and terrors so unmanning; and you can do but one thing, Utterson, to lighten this destiny, and that is to respect my silence." Utterson was amazed; the dark influence of Hyde had been withdrawn, the doctor had returned to his old tasks and amities; a week ago, the prospect had smiled with every promise of a cheerful and an honoured age; and now in a moment, friendship and peace of mind and the whole tenor of his life were wrecked. So great and unprepared a change pointed to madness; but in view of Lanyon's manner and words, there must lie for it some deeper ground.

A week afterwards Dr. Lanyon took to his bed, and in something less than a fortnight he was dead. The night after the funeral, at which he had been sadly affected, Utterson locked the door of his business room, and sitting there by the light of a melancholy candle, drew out and set before him an envelope addressed by the hand and sealed with the seal of his dead friend. "PRIVATE: for the hands of J. G. Utterson ALONE, and in case of his predecease *to be destroyed unread*," so it was emphatically superscribed; and the lawyer dreaded to behold the contents. "I have buried one friend to-day," he thought: "what if this should cost me another?" And then he condemned the fear as a disloyalty, and broke the seal. Within there was another enclosure, likewise sealed, and marked upon the cover as "not to be opened till the death or disappearance of Dr. Henry Jekyll." Utterson could not trust his eyes. Yes, it was disappearance; here again, as in the mad will, which he had long ago restored to its author, here again were the idea of a disappearance and the name of Henry Jekyll bracketed. But in the will, that idea had sprung from the sinister suggestion of the man Hyde; it was set there with a purpose all too plain and horrible. Written by the hand of Lanyon, what should it mean? A great curiosity came to the trustee, to disregard the prohibition and dive at once to the bottom of these mysteries; but professional honour and faith to his dead friend were stringent obligations; and the packet slept in the inmost corner of his private safe.

It is one thing to mortify curiosity, another to conquer it; and it may be doubted if, from that day forth, Utterson desired the society of his surviving friend with the same eagerness. He thought of him kindly; but his thoughts were disquieted and fearful. He went to call indeed; but he was perhaps relieved to be denied admittance; perhaps, in his heart, he preferred to speak with Poole upon the doorstep, and surrounded by the air and sounds of the open city, rather than to be admitted into that house of voluntary bondage, and to sit and speak with its inscrutable recluse. Poole had, indeed, no very pleasant news to communicate. The doctor, it appeared, now more than ever confined himself to the cabinet over the laboratory, where he would sometimes even sleep; he was out of spirits, he had grown very silent, he did not read; it seemed as if he had something on his mind. Utterson became so used to the unvarying character of these reports, that he fell off little by little in the frequency of his visits.

Incident at the Window

It chanced on Sunday, when Mr. Utterson was on his usual walk with Mr. Enfield, that their way lay once again through the by street; and that when they came in front of the door, both stopped to gaze on it.

"Well," said Enfield, "that story's at an end, at least. We shall never see more of Mr. Hyde."

"I hope not," said Utterson. "Did I ever tell you that I once saw him, and shared your feeling of repulsion?"

"It was impossible to do the one without the other," returned Enfield. "And, by the way, what an ass you must have thought me, not to know that this was a back way to Dr. Jekyll's! It was partly your own fault that I found it out, even when I did."

"So you found it out, did you?" said Utterson. "But if that be so, we may step into the court and take a look at the windows. To tell you the truth, I am uneasy about poor Jekyll; and even outside, I feel as if the presence of a friend might do him good."

The court was very cool and a little damp, and full of

premature twilight, although the sky, high up overhead, was still bright with sunset. The middle one of the three windows was half way open; and sitting close beside it, taking the air with an infinite sadness of mien, like some disconsolate prisoner, Utterson saw Dr. Jekyll.

"What! Jekyll!" he cried. "I trust you are better."

"I am very low, Utterson," replied the doctor drearily; "very low. It will not last long, thank God."

"You stay too much indoors," said the lawyer. "You should be out, whipping up the circulation like Mr. Enfield and me. (This is my cousin—Mr. Enfield—Dr. Jekyll.) Come, now; get your hat and take a quick turn with us."

"You are very good," sighed the other. "I should like to very much; but no, no, no, it is quite impossible; I dare not. But indeed, Utterson, I am very glad to see you; this is really a great pleasure. I would ask you and Mr. Enfield up, but the place is really not fit."

"Why then," said the lawyer, good-naturedly, "the best thing we can do is to stay down here, and speak with you from where we are."

"That is just what I was about to venture to propose," returned the doctor, with a smile. But the words were hardly uttered, before the smile was struck out of his face and succeeded by an expression of such abject terror and despair, as froze the very blood of the two gentlemen below. They saw it but for a glimpse, for the window was instantly thrust down; but that glimpse had been sufficient, and they turned and left the court without a word. In silence, too, they traversed the by street; and it was not until they had come into a neighbouring thoroughfare, where even upon a Sunday there were still some stirrings of life, that Mr. Utterson at last turned and looked at his companion. They were both pale; and there was an answering horror in their eyes.

"God forgive us! God forgive us!" said Mr. Utterson.

But Mr. Enfield only nodded his head very seriously, and walked on once more in silence.

THE LAST NIGHT

M r. Utterson was sitting by his fireside one evening after dinner, when he was surprised to receive a visit from Poole.

"Bless me, Poole, what brings you here?" he cried; and then, taking a second look at him, "What ails you?" he added; "is the doctor ill?"

"Mr. Utterson," said the man, "there is something wrong."

"Take a seat, and here is a glass of wine for you," said the lawyer. "Now, take your time, and tell me plainly what you want."

"You know the doctor's ways, sir," replied Poole, "and how he shuts himself up. Well, he's shut up again in the cabinet; and I don't like it, sir—I wish I may die if I like it. Mr. Utterson, sir, I'm afraid."

"Now, my good man," said the lawyer, "be explicit. What are you afraid of?"

"I've been afraid for about a week," returned Poole,

doggedly disregarding the question, "and I can bear it no more."

The man's appearance amply bore out his words; his manner was altered for the worse; and except for the moment when he had first announced his terror, he had not once looked the lawyer in the face. Even now, he sat with the glass of wine untasted on his knee, and his eyes directed to a corner of the floor. "I can bear it no more," he repeated.

"Come," said the lawyer, "I see you have some good reason, Poole; I see there is something seriously amiss. Try to tell me what it is."

"I think there's been foul play," said Poole, hoarsely.

"Foul play!" cried the lawyer, a good deal frightened, and rather inclined to be irritated in consequence. "What foul play? What does the man mean?"

"I daren't say, sir," was the answer; "but will you come along with me and see for yourself?"

Mr. Utterson's only answer was to rise and get his hat and great coat; but he observed with wonder the greatness of the relief that appeared upon the butler's face, and perhaps with no less, that the wine was still untasted when he set it down to follow.

It was a wild, cold, seasonable night of March, with a pale moon, lying on her back as though the wind had tilted her, and a flying wrack[1] of the most diaphanous and lawny[2] texture. The wind made talking difficult, and flecked the blood into the face. It seemed to have swept the streets unusually bare of passengers, besides; for Mr. Utterson thought he had never seen that part of London so deserted. He could have wished it otherwise; never in his life had he been conscious of so sharp a wish to see and touch his fellow-creatures; for, struggle as he might, there was borne in upon his mind a crushing anticipation of calamity. The square, when they got there, was all full of wind and dust, and the thin trees in the garden were lashing themselves along the railing. Poole, who had kept all the way a pace or two ahead, now pulled up in the middle of the pavement, and in spite of the biting weather, took off his hat and mopped his brow with a red pocket-handkerchief. But for all the hurry of his coming, these were not the dews of exertion that he wiped away, but the moisture of some strangling anguish; for his face was white, and his voice, when he spoke, harsh and broken.

"Well, sir," he said, "here we are, and God grant there be nothing wrong."

"Amen, Poole," said the lawyer.

Thereupon the servant knocked in a very guarded manner; the door was opened on the chain; and a voice asked from within, "Is that you, Poole?"

"It's all right," said Poole. "Open the door."

The hall, when they entered it, was brightly lighted up; the fire was built high; and about the hearth the whole of the servants, men and women, stood huddled together like a flock of sheep. At the sight of Mr. Utterson, the housemaid broke into hysterical whimpering; and the cook, crying out, "Bless God! it's Mr. Utterson," ran forward as if to take him in her arms.

"What, what? Are you all here?" said the lawyer, peevishly. "Very irregular, very unseemly: your master would be far from pleased."

"They're all afraid," said Poole.

Blank silence followed, no one protesting; only the maid lifted up her voice and now wept loudly.

"Hold your tongue!" Poole said to her, with a ferocity

of accent that testified to his own jangled nerves; and indeed when the girl had so suddenly raised the note of her lamentation, they had all started and turned towards the inner door with faces of dreadful expectation. "And now," continued the butler, addressing the knife-boy, "reach me a candle, and we'll get this through hands at once." And then he begged Mr. Utterson to follow him, and led the way to the back garden.

"Now, sir," said he, "you come as gently as you can. I want you to hear, and I don't want you to be heard. And see here, sir, if by any chance he was to ask you in, don't go."

Mr. Utterson's nerves, at this unlooked-for termination, gave a jerk that nearly threw him from his balance; but he re-collected his courage, and followed the butler into the laboratory building and through the surgical theatre, with its lumber of crates and bottles, to the foot of the stair. Here Poole motioned him to stand on one side and listen; while he himself, setting down the candle and making a great and obvious call on his resolution, mounted the steps, and knocked with a somewhat uncertain hand on the red baize of the cabinet door.

"Mr. Utterson, sir, asking to see you," he called; and even as he did so, once more violently signed to the lawyer to give ear.

A voice answered from within: "Tell him I cannot see any one," it said, complainingly.

"Thank you, sir," said Poole, with a note of something like triumph in his voice; and taking up his candle, he led Mr. Utterson back across the yard and into the great kitchen, where the fire was out and the beetles were leaping on the floor.

"Sir," he said, looking Mr. Utterson in the eyes, "was that my master's voice?"

"It seems much changed," replied the lawyer, very pale, but giving look for look.

"Changed? Well, yes, I think so," said the butler. "Have I been twenty years in this man's house, to be deceived about his voice? No, sir; master's made away with; he was made away with eight days ago, when we heard him cry out upon the name of God; and *who's* in there instead of him, and *why* it stays there, is a thing that cries to Heaven, Mr. Utterson!"

"This is a very strange tale, Poole; this is rather a wild tale, my man," said Mr. Utterson, biting his finger. "Suppose it were as you suppose, supposing Dr. Jekyll to have been—well, murdered, what could induce the murderer to stay? That won't hold water; it doesn't commend itself to reason."

"Well, Mr. Utterson, you are a hard man to satisfy, but I'll do it yet," said Poole. "All this last week (you must know) him, or it, or whatever it is that lives in that cabinet, has been crying night and day for some sort of medicine and cannot get it to his mind. It was sometimes his way—the master's, that is—to write his orders on a sheet of paper and throw it on the stair. We've had nothing else this week back; nothing but papers, and a closed door, and the very meals left there to be smuggled in when nobody was looking. Well, sir, every day, ay, and twice and thrice in the same day, there have been orders and complaints, and I have been sent flying to all the wholesale chemists in town. Every time I brought the stuff back, there would be another paper telling me to return it, because it was not pure, and another order to a different firm. This drug is wanted bitter bad, sir, whatever for."

"Have you any of these papers?" asked Mr. Utterson.

Poole felt in his pocket and handed out a crumpled note, which the lawyer, bending nearer to the candle, carefully examined. Its contents ran thus: "Dr. Jekyll presents his compliments to Messrs. Maw. He assures them that their last sample is impure and quite useless for his present purpose. In the year 18——, Dr. J. purchased a somewhat large quantity from Messrs. M. He now begs them to search with the most sedulous care, and should any of the same quality be left, to forward it to him at once. Expense is no consideration. The importance of this to Dr. J. can hardly be exaggerated." So far the letter had run composedly enough; but here, with a sudden splutter of the pen, the writer's emotion had broken loose. "For God's sake," he had added, "find me some of the old."

"This is a strange note," said Mr. Utterson; and then sharply, "How do you come to have it open?"

"The man at Maw's was main angry, sir, and he threw it back to me like so much dirt," returned Poole.

"This is unquestionably the doctor's hand, do you know?" resumed the lawyer.

"I thought it looked like it," said the servant, rather sulkily; and then, with another voice, "But what matters hand of write?" he said. "I've seen him!"

"Seen him?" repeated Mr. Utterson. "Well?"

"That's it!" said Poole. "It was this way. I came suddenly into the theatre from the garden. It seems he had slipped out to look for this drug, or whatever it is; for the cabinet door was open, and there he was at the far end of the room digging among the crates. He looked up when I came in, gave a kind of cry, and whipped upstairs into the cabinet. It was but for one minute that I saw him, but the hair stood upon my head like quills. Sir, if that was my master, why had he a mask upon his face? If it was my master, why did he cry out like a rat and run from me? I have served him long enough. And then . . ." the man paused and passed his hand over his face.

"These are all very strange circumstances," said Mr. Utterson, "but I think I begin to see daylight. Your master, Poole, is plainly seized with one of those maladies that both torture and deform the sufferer; hence, for aught I know, the alteration of his voice; hence the mask and his avoidance of his friends; hence his eagerness to find this drug, by means of which the poor soul retains some hope of ultimate recovery—God grant that he be not deceived! There is my explanation; it is sad enough, Poole, ay, and appalling to consider; but it is plain and natural, hangs well together and delivers us from all exorbitant alarms."

"Sir," said the butler, turning to a sort of mottled pallor, "that thing was not my master, and there's the truth. My master"—here he looked round him, and began to whisper—"is a tall fine build of a man, and this was more of a dwarf." Utterson attempted to protest. "O, sir," cried Poole, "do you think I do not know my master after twenty years? do you think I do not know where his head comes to in the cabinet door, where I saw him every morning of my life? No, sir, that thing in the mask was never Dr. Jekyll—God knows what it was, but it was never Dr. Jekyll; and it is the belief of my heart that there was murder done."

"Poole," replied the lawyer, "if you say that, it will become my duty to make certain. Much as I desire to spare your master's feelings, much as I am puzzled about this note, which seems to prove him to be still alive, I shall consider it my duty to break in that door."

"Ah, Mr. Utterson, that's talking!" cried the butler.

"And now comes the second question," resumed Utterson: "Who is going to do it?"

"Why, you and me, sir," was the undaunted reply.

"That is very well said," returned the lawyer; "and whatever comes of it, I shall make it my business to see you are no loser."

"There is an axe in the theatre," continued Poole; "and you might take the kitchen poker for yourself."

The lawyer took that rude but weighty instrument into his hand, and balanced it. "Do you know, Poole," he said, looking up, "that you and I are about to place ourselves in a position of some peril?"

"You may say so, sir, indeed," returned the butler.

"It is well, then, that we should be frank," said the other. "We both think more than we have said; let us make a clean breast. This masked figure that you saw, did you recognise it?"

"Well, sir, it went so quick, and the creature was so doubled up, that I could hardly swear to that," was the answer. "But if you mean, was it Mr. Hyde?—why, yes, I think it was! You see, it was much of the same bigness; and it had the same quick light way with it; and then who else could have got in by the laboratory door? You have not forgot, sir, that at the time of the murder he had still the key with him? But that's not all. I don't know, Mr. Utterson, if ever you met this Mr. Hyde?"

"Yes," said the lawyer, "I once spoke with him."

"Then you must know, as well as the rest of us, that there was something queer about that gentleman— something that gave a man a turn—I don't know rightly how to say it, sir, beyond this: that you felt in your marrow—kind of cold and thin."

"I own I felt something of what you describe," said Mr. Utterson.

"Quite so, sir," returned Poole. "Well, when that masked thing like a monkey jumped up from among the chemicals and whipped into the cabinet, it went down my spine like ice. O, I know it's not evidence, Mr. Utterson; I'm book-learned enough for that; but a man has his feelings; and I give you my bible-word it was Mr. Hyde!"

"Ay, ay," said the lawyer. "My fears incline to the same point. Evil, I fear, founded—evil was sure to come—of that connection. Ay, truly, I believe you; I believe poor Harry is killed; and I believe his murderer (for what purpose, God alone can tell) is still lurking in his victim's room. Well, let our name be vengeance. Call Bradshaw."

The footman came at the summons, very white and nervous.

"Pull yourself together, Bradshaw," said the lawyer. "This suspense, I know, is telling upon all of you; but it is now our intention to make an end of it. Poole, here, and I are going to force our way into the cabinet. If all is well, my shoulders are broad enough to bear the blame. Meanwhile, lest anything should really be amiss, or any malefactor seek to escape by the back, you and the boy must go round the corner with a pair of good sticks, and take your post at the laboratory door. We give you ten minutes, to get to your stations."

As Bradshaw left, the lawyer looked at his watch. "And now, Poole, let us get to ours," he said; and taking the poker under his arm, he led the way into the yard. The scud had banked over the moon, and it was now quite dark. The wind, which only broke in puffs and draughts into that deep well of building, tossed the light of the candle to and fro about their steps, until they came into the shelter of the theatre, where they sat down silently to wait. London hummed solemnly all around; but nearer at hand, the stillness was only broken by the sound of a footfall moving to and fro along the cabinet floor.

"So it will walk all day, sir," whispered Poole; "ay, and the better part of the night. Only when a new sample comes from the chemist, there's a bit of a break. Ah, it's an ill conscience that's such an enemy to rest! Ah, sir, there's blood foully shed in every step of it! But hark again, a little closer—put your heart in your ears Mr. Utterson, and tell me, is that the doctor's foot?"

The steps fell lightly and oddly, with a certain swing, for all they went so slowly; it was different indeed from the heavy creaking tread of Henry Jekyll. Utterson sighed. "Is there never anything else?" he asked.

Poole nodded. "Once," he said. "Once I heard it weeping!"

"Weeping? how that?" said the lawyer, conscious of a sudden chill of horror.

"Weeping like a woman or a lost soul," said the butler. "I came away with that upon my heart, that I could have wept too."

But now the ten minutes drew to an end. Poole disinterred the axe from under a stack of packing straw; the candle was set upon the nearest table to light them to the attack; and they drew near with bated breath to where the patient foot was still going up and down, up and down in the quiet of the night.

"Jekyll," cried Utterson, with a loud voice, "I demand to see you." He paused a moment, but there came no reply. "I give you fair warning, our suspicions are aroused, and I must and shall see you," he resumed; "if not by fair means, then by foul—if not of your consent, then by brute force!"

"Utterson," said the voice, "for God's sake, have mercy!"

"Ah, that's not Jekyll's voice—it's Hyde's!" cried Utterson. "Down with the door, Poole!"

Poole swung the axe over his shoulder; the blow shook the building, and the red baize door leaped against the lock and hinges. A dismal screech, as of mere animal terror, rang from the cabinet. Up went the axe again, and again the panels crashed and the frame bounded; four times the blow fell; but the wood was tough and the fittings were of excellent workmanship; and it was not until the fifth that the lock burst in sunder, and the wreck of the door fell inwards on the carpet.

The besiegers, appalled by their own riot and the stillness that had succeeded, stood back a little and peered in. There lay the cabinet before their eyes in the quiet lamplight, a good fire glowing and chattering on the hearth, the kettle singing its thin strain, a drawer or two open, papers neatly set forth on the business table, and nearer the fire, the things laid out for tea; the quietest room, you would have said, and, but for the glazed presses full of chemicals, the most commonplace that night in London.

Right in the midst there lay the body of a man sorely contorted and still twitching. They drew near on tiptoe, turned it on its back, and beheld the face of Edward Hyde. He was dressed in clothes far too large for him, clothes of the doctor's bigness; the cords of his face still moved with a semblance of life, but life was quite gone;

and by the crushed phial in the hand and the strong smell of kernels[3] that hung upon the air, Utterson knew that he was looking on the body of a self-destroyer.

"We have come too late," he said sternly, "whether to save or punish. Hyde is gone to his account; and it only remains for us to find the body of your master."

The far greater proportion of the building was occupied by the theatre, which filled almost the whole ground storey, and was lighted from above, and by the cabinet, which formed an upper storey at one end and looked upon the court. A corridor joined the theatre to the door on the by street; and with this, the cabinet communicated separately by a second flight of stairs. There were besides a few dark closets and a spacious cellar. All these they now thoroughly examined. Each closet needed but a glance, for all they were empty and all, by the dust that fell from their doors, had stood long unopened. The cellar, indeed, was filled with crazy lumber, mostly dating from the times of the surgeon who was Jekyll's predecessor; but even as they opened the door, they were advertised of the uselessness of further search by the fall of a perfect mat of cobweb which had for years sealed up the entrance. Nowhere was there any trace of Henry Jekyll, dead or alive.

Poole stamped on the flags of the corridor. "He must be buried here," he said, hearkening to the sound.

"Or he may have fled," said Utterson, and he turned to examine the door in the by street. It was locked; and lying near by on the flags, they found the key, already stained with rust.

"This does not look like use," observed the lawyer.

"Use!" echoed Poole. "Do you not see, sir, it is broken? much as if a man had stamped on it."

"Ah," continued Utterson, "and the fractures, too, are rusty." The two men looked at each other with a scare. "This is beyond me, Poole," said the lawyer. "Let us go back to the cabinet."

They mounted the stair in silence, and still, with an occasional awestruck glance at the dead body, proceeded more thoroughly to examine the contents of the cabinet. At one table, there were traces of chemical work, various measured heaps of some white salt being laid on glass saucers, as though for an experiment in which the unhappy man had been prevented.

"That is the same drug that I was always bringing him," said Poole; and even as he spoke, the kettle with a startling noise boiled over.

This brought them to the fireside, where the easy chair was drawn cosily up, and the tea things stood ready to the sitter's elbow, the very sugar in the cup. There were several books on a shelf; one lay beside the tea things open, and Utterson was amazed to find it a copy of a pious work for which Jekyll had several times expressed a great esteem, annotated, in his own hand, with startling blasphemies.

Next, in the course of their review of the chamber, the searchers came to the cheval-glass, into whose depth they looked with an involuntary horror. But it was so turned as to show them nothing but the rosy glow playing on the roof, the fire sparkling in a hundred repetitions along the glazed front of the presses, and their own pale and fearful countenances stooping to look in.

"This glass has seen some strange things, sir," whispered Poole.

"And surely none stranger than itself," echoed the lawyer, in the same tone. "For what did Jekyll"—he caught himself up at the word with a start, and then conquering the weakness: "what could Jekyll want with it?" he said.

"You may say that!" said Poole.

Next they turned to the business table. On the desk, among the neat array of papers, a large envelope was uppermost, and bore, in the doctor's hand, the name of Mr. Utterson. The lawyer unsealed it, and several enclosures fell to the floor. The first was a will, drawn in the same eccentric terms as the one which he had returned six months before, to serve as a testament in case of death and as a deed of gift in case of disappearance; but in place of the name of Edward Hyde, the lawyer, with indescribable amazement, read the name of Gabriel John Utterson. He looked at Poole, and then back at the papers, and last of all at the dead malefactor stretched upon the carpet.

"My head goes round," he said. "He has been all these days in possession; he had no cause to like me; he must have raged to see himself displaced; and he has not destroyed this document."

He caught the next paper; it was a brief note in the doctor's hand and dated at the top. "O Poole!" the lawyer cried, "he was alive and here this day. He cannot have been disposed of in so short a space; he must be still alive, he must have fled! And then, why fled? and how? and in that case can we venture to declare this suicide? O, we must be careful. I foresee that we may yet involve your master in some dire catastrophe."

"Why don't you read it, sir?" asked Poole.

"Because I fear," replied the lawyer, solemnly. "God grant I have no cause for it!" And with that he brought the paper to his eyes, and read as follows:

My dear Utterson,—When this shall fall into your hands, I shall have disappeared, under what circumstances I have not the penetration to foresee, but my instinct and all the circumstances of my nameless situation tell me that the end is sure and must be early. Go then, and first read the narrative which Lanyon warned me he was to place in your hands; and if you care to hear more, turn to the confession of

Your unworthy and unhappy friend,
Henry Jekyll

"There was a third enclosure," asked Utterson.

"Here, sir," said Poole, and gave into his hands a considerable packet sealed in several places.

The lawyer put it in his pocket. "I would say nothing of this paper. If your master has fled or is dead, we may at least save his credit. It is now ten; I must go home and read these documents in quiet; but I shall be back before midnight, when we shall send for the police."

They went out, locking the door of the theatre behind them; and Utterson, once more leaving the servants gathered about the fire in the hall, trudged back to his office to read the two narratives in which this mystery was now to be explained.

Dr. Lanyon's Narrative

On the ninth of January, now four days ago, I received by the evening delivery a registered envelope, addressed in the hand of my colleague and old school-companion, Henry Jekyll. I was a good deal surprised by this; for we were by no means in the habit of correspondence; I had seen the man, dined with him, indeed, the night before; and I could imagine nothing in our intercourse that should justify the formality of registration. The contents increased my wonder; for this is how the letter ran:

10th December 18[1]——

Dear Lanyon,—You are one of my oldest friends; and although we may have differed at times on scientific questions, I cannot remember, at least on my side, any break in our affection. There was never a day when, if you had said to me, "Jekyll, my life, my honour, my reason, depend upon you," I would not have sacrificed my fortune or my left hand to help you. Lanyon, my life, my honour, my reason, are all at your mercy; if you fail me to-night, I am lost. You might suppose, after this preface, that I am going to ask you for something dishonourable to grant. Judge for yourself.

I want you to postpone all other engagements for to-night—ay, even if you were summoned to the bedside of an emperor; to take a cab, unless your carriage should be actually at the door; and, with this letter in your hand for consultation, to drive straight to my house. Poole, my butler, has his orders; you will find him waiting your arrival with a locksmith. The door of my cabinet is then to be forced; and you are to go in alone; to open the glazed press (letter E) on the left hand, breaking the lock if it be shut; and to draw out, *with all its contents as they stand,* the fourth drawer from the top or (which is the same thing) the third from the bottom. In my extreme distress of mind, I have a morbid fear of misdirecting you; but even if I am in error, you may know the right drawer by its contents: some powders, a phial, and a paper book. This drawer I beg of you to carry back with you to Cavendish Square exactly as it stands.

That is the first part of the service: now for the second. You should be back, if you set out at once on the receipt of this, long before midnight; but I will leave you that amount of margin, not only in the fear of one of those obstacles that can neither be prevented nor foreseen, but because an hour when your servants are in bed is to be preferred for what will then remain to do. At midnight, then, I have to ask you to be alone in your consulting-room, to admit with your own hand into the house a man who will present himself in my name, and to place in his hands the drawer that you will have brought with you from my cabinet. Then you will have played your part and earned my gratitude completely. Five minutes afterwards, if you insist upon an explanation, you will have understood that these arrangements are of capital importance; and that by the neglect of one of them, fantastic as they must appear, you might have charged your conscience with my death or the shipwreck of my reason.

Confident as I am that you will not trifle with this appeal, my heart sinks and my hand trembles at the bare thought of such a possibility. Think of me at this hour, in a strange place, labouring under a blackness of distress that no fancy can exaggerate, and yet well aware that, if you will but punctually serve me, my troubles will roll away like a story that is told. Serve me, my dear Lanyon, and save

Your friend,
H.J.

PS.—I had already sealed this up when a fresh terror struck upon my soul. It is possible that the post office may fail me, and this letter not come into your hands until to-morrow morning. In that case, dear Lanyon, do my errand when it shall be most convenient for you in the course of the day; and once more expect my messenger at midnight. It may then already be too late; and if that night passes without event, you will know that you have seen the last of Henry Jekyll.

Upon the reading of this letter, I made sure my colleague was insane; but till that was proved beyond the possibility of doubt, I felt bound to do as he requested. The less I understood of this farrago, the less I was in a position to judge of its importance; and an appeal so worded could not be set aside without a grave responsibility. I rose accordingly from table, got into a hansom, and drove straight to Jekyll's house. The butler was awaiting my arrival; he had received by the same post as mine a registered letter of instruction, and had sent at once for a locksmith and a carpenter. The tradesmen came while we were yet speaking; and we moved in a body to old Dr. Denman's surgical theatre, from which (as you are doubtless aware) Jekyll's private cabinet is most conveniently entered. The door was very strong, the lock excellent; the carpenter avowed he would have great trouble, and have to do much damage, if force were to be used; and the locksmith was near despair. But this last was a handy fellow, and after two hours' work, the door stood open. The press marked E was unlocked; and I took out the drawer, had it filled up with straw and tied in a sheet, and returned with it to Cavendish Square.

Here I proceeded to examine its contents. The powders were neatly enough made up, but not with the nicety of the dispensing chemist; so that it was plain they were of Jekyll's private manufacture; and when I opened one of the wrappers, I found what seemed to me a simple crystalline salt of a white colour. The phial, to which I next turned my attention, might have been about half-full of a blood-red liquor, which was highly pungent to the sense of smell, and seemed to me to contain phosphorus and some volatile ether. At the other ingredients I could make no guess. The book was an ordinary version book, and contained little but a series of dates. These covered a period of many years, but I observed that the entries ceased nearly a year ago and quite abruptly. Here and there a brief remark was appended to a date, usually no more than a single word: "double" occurring perhaps six times in a total of several hundred entries; and once very early in the list and followed by several marks of exclamation, "total failure!!!" All this, though it whetted my curiosity, told me little that was definite. Here were a phial of some tincture, a paper of some salt, and the record of a series of experiments that had led (like too many of Jekyll's investigations) to no end of practical usefulness. How could the presence of these articles in my house affect either the honour, the sanity, or the life of my flighty colleague? If his messenger could go to one place, why could he not go to another? And even granting some impediment, why was this gentleman to be received by me in secret? The more I reflected, the more convinced I grew that I was dealing with a case of cerebral disease; and though I dismissed my servants to bed, I loaded an old revolver, that I might be found in some posture of self-defence.

Twelve o'clock had scarce rung out over London, ere the knocker sounded very gently on the door. I went myself at the summons, and found a small man crouching against the pillars of the portico.

"Are you come from Dr. Jekyll?" I asked.

He told me "yes" by a constrained gesture; and when I had bidden him enter, he did not obey me without a searching backward glance into the darkness of the square. There was a policeman not far off, advancing

with his bull's eye open;[2] and at the sight, I thought my
visitor started and made greater haste.

These particulars struck me, I confess, disagreeably;
and as I followed him into the bright light of the
consulting-room, I kept my hand ready on my weapon.
Here, at last, I had a chance of clearly seeing him. I had
never set eyes on him before, so much was certain. He
was small, as I have said; I was struck besides with the
shocking expression of his face, with his remarkable
combination of great muscular activity and great appar-
ent debility of constitution, and—last but not least—
with the odd, subjective disturbance caused by his
neighbourhood. This bore some resemblance to incipi-
ent rigor, and was accompanied by a marked sinking of
the pulse. At the time, I set it down to some idiosyn-
cratic, personal distaste, and merely wondered at the
acuteness of the symptoms; but I have since had reason
to believe the cause to lie much deeper in the nature of
man, and to turn on some nobler hinge than the princi-
ple of hatred.

This person (who had thus, from the first moment of
his entrance, struck in me what I can only describe as a
disgustful curiosity) was dressed in a fashion that would
have made an ordinary person laughable; his clothes,
that is to say, although they were of rich and sober fabric, were enormously too large for him in every mea-
surement—the trousers hanging on his legs and rolled
up to keep them from the ground, the waist of the coat
below his haunches, and the collar sprawling wide upon
his shoulders. Strange to relate, this ludicrous accou-
trement was far from moving me to laughter. Rather, as
there was something abnormal and misbegotten in the
very essence of the creature that now faced me—some-

thing seizing, surprising and revolting—this fresh disparity seemed but to fit in with and to reinforce it; so that to my interest in the man's nature and character there was added a curiosity as to his origin, his life, his fortune and status in the world.

These observations, though they have taken so great a space to be set down in, were yet the work of a few seconds. My visitor was, indeed, on fire with sombre excitement.

"Have you got it?" he cried. "Have you got it?" And so lively was his impatience that he even laid his hand upon my arm and sought to shake me.

I put him back, conscious at his touch of a certain icy pang along my blood. "Come, sir," said I. "You forget that I have not yet the pleasure of your acquaintance. Be seated, if you please." And I showed him an example, and sat down myself in my customary seat and with as fair an imitation of my ordinary manner to a patient, as the lateness of the hour, the nature of my preoccupations, and the horror I had of my visitor would suffer me to muster.

"I beg your pardon, Dr. Lanyon," he replied, civilly enough. "What you say is very well founded; and my impatience has shown its heels to my politeness. I come here at the instance of your colleague, Dr. Henry Jekyll, on a piece of business of some moment; and I understood . . ." he paused and put his hand to his throat, and I could see, in spite of his collected manner, that he was wrestling against the approaches of the hysteria—"I understood, a drawer . . ."

But here I took pity on my visitor's suspense, and some perhaps on my own growing curiosity.

"There it is, sir," said I, pointing to the drawer where

it lay on the floor behind a table, and still covered with the sheet.

He sprang to it, and then paused, and laid his hand upon his heart; I could hear his teeth grate with the convulsive action of his jaws; and his face was so ghastly to see that I grew alarmed both for his life and reason.

"Compose yourself," said I.

He turned a dreadful smile to me, and, as if with the decision of despair, plucked away the sheet. At sight of the contents, he uttered one loud sob of such immense relief that I sat petrified. And the next moment, in a voice that was already fairly well under control, "Have you a graduated glass?" he asked.

I rose from my place with something of an effort, and gave him what he asked.

He thanked me with a smiling nod, measured out a few minims of the red tincture and added one of the powders. The mixture, which was at first of a reddish hue, began, in proportion as the crystals melted, to brighten in colour, to effervesce audibly, and to throw off small fumes of vapour. Suddenly, and at the same moment, the ebullition ceased, and the compound changed to a dark purple, which faded again more slowly to a watery green. My visitor, who had watched these metamorphoses with a keen eye, smiled, set down the glass upon the table, and then turned and looked upon me with an air of scrutiny.

"And now," said he, "to settle what remains. Will you be wise? will you be guided? will you suffer me to take this glass in my hand, and to go forth from your house without further parley? or has the greed of curiosity too much command of you? Think before you answer, for it shall be done as you decide. As you decide, you shall be left as you were before, and neither richer nor wiser, unless the sense of service rendered to a man in mortal distress may be counted as a kind of riches of the soul. Or, if you shall so prefer to choose, a new province of knowledge and new avenues to fame and power shall be laid open to you, here, in this room, upon the instant; and your sight shall be blasted by a prodigy to stagger the unbelief of Satan."

"Sir," said I, affecting a coolness that I was far from truly possessing, "you speak enigmas, and you will perhaps not wonder that I hear you with no very strong impression of belief. But I have gone too far in the way of inexplicable services to pause before I see the end."

"It is well," replied my visitor. "Lanyon, you remember your vows: what follows is under the seal of our profession. And now, you who have so long been bound to the most narrow and material views, you who have denied the virtue of transcendental medicine, you who have derided your superiors—behold!"

He put the glass to his lips, and drank at one gulp. A cry followed; he reeled, staggered, clutched at the table and held on, staring with injected eyes, gasping with open mouth; and as I looked, there came, I thought, a change—he seemed to swell—his face became suddenly black, and the features seemed to melt and alter—and the next moment I had sprung to my feet and leaped back against the wall, my arm raised to shield me from that prodigy, my mind submerged in terror.

"O God!" I screamed, and "O God!" again and again; for there before my eyes—pale and shaken, and half fainting, and groping before him with his hands, like a man restored from death—there stood Henry Jekyll!

What he told me in the next hour I cannot bring my mind to set on paper. I saw what I saw, I heard what I heard, and my soul sickened at it; and yet, now when that sight has faded from my eyes, I ask myself if I believe it, and I cannot answer. My life is shaken to its roots; sleep has left me; the deadliest terror sits by me at all hours of the day and night; I feel that my days are numbered, and that I must die; and yet I shall die incredulous. As for the moral turpitude that man unveiled to me, even with tears of penitence, I cannot, even in memory, dwell on it without a start of horror. I will say but one thing, Utterson, and that (if you can bring your mind to credit it) will be more than enough. The creature who crept into my house that night was, on Jekyll's own confession, known by the name of Hyde and hunted for in every corner of the land as the murderer of Carew.

Hastie Lanyon

HENRY JEKYLL'S FULL STATEMENT
OF THE CASE

I was born in the year 18——to a large fortune, en-
dowed besides with excellent parts, inclined by nature to industry, fond of the respect of the wise and
good among my fellow-men, and thus, as might have
been supposed, with every guarantee of an honourable
and distinguished future. And indeed, the worst of my
faults was a certain impatient gaiety of disposition, such
as has made the happiness of many, but such as I found
it hard to reconcile with my imperious desire to carry
my head high, and wear a more than commonly grave
countenance before the public. Hence it came about
that I concealed my pleasures; and that when I reached
years of reflection, and began to look round me and
take stock of my progress and position in the world, I
stood already committed to a profound duplicity of life.
Many a man would have even blazoned such irregulari-
ties as I was guilty of; but from the high views that I had
set before me, I regarded and hid them with an almost
morbid sense of shame. It was thus rather the exacting

nature of my aspirations, than any particular degradation in my faults, that made me what I was and, with even a deeper trench than in the majority of men, severed in me those provinces of good and ill which divide and compound man's dual nature. In this case, I was driven to reflect deeply and inveterately on that hard law of life which lies at the root of religion, and is one of the most plentiful springs of distress. Though so profound a double-dealer, I was in no sense a hypocrite; both sides of me were in dead earnest; I was no more myself when I laid aside restraint and plunged in shame, than when I laboured, in the eye of day, at the furtherance of knowledge or the relief of sorrow and suffering. And it chanced that the direction of my scientific studies, which led wholly towards the mystic and the transcendental, reacted and shed a strong light on this consciousness of the perennial war among my members.[1] With every day, and from both sides of my intelligence, the moral and the intellectual, I thus drew steadily nearer to that truth by whose partial discovery I have been doomed to such a dreadful shipwreck: that man is not truly one, but truly two. I say two, because the state of my own knowledge does not pass beyond that point. Others will follow, others will outstrip me on the same lines; and I hazard the guess that man will be ultimately known for a mere polity of multifarious, incongruous and independent denizens. I, for my part, from the nature of my life, advanced infallibly in one direction and in one direction only. It was on the moral side, and in my own person, that I learned to recognise the thorough and primitive duality of man; I saw that, of the two natures that contended in the field of my consciousness, even if I could rightly be said to be either, it was only because I was radically both; and from an early date, even before the course of my scientific discoveries had begun to suggest the most naked possibility of such a miracle, I had learned to dwell with pleasure, as a beloved daydream, on the thought of the separation of these elements. If each, I told myself, could but be housed in separate identities, life would be relieved of all that was unbearable; the unjust might go his way, delivered from the aspirations and remorse of his more upright twin; and the just could walk steadfastly and securely on his upward path, doing the good things in which he found his pleasure, and no longer exposed to disgrace and penitence by the hands of this extraneous evil. It was the curse of mankind that these incongruous faggots were thus bound together—that in the agonised womb of consciousness these polar twins should be continuously struggling. How, then, were they dissociated?

I was so far in my reflections when, as I have said, a side light began to shine upon the subject from the laboratory table. I began to perceive more deeply than it has ever yet been stated, the trembling immateriality, the mist-like transience, of this seemingly so solid body in which we walk attired. Certain agents I found to have the power to shake and to pluck back that fleshly vestment, even as a wind might toss the curtains of a pavilion. For two good reasons, I will not enter deeply into this scientific branch of my confession. First, because I have been made to learn that the doom and burthen of our life is bound for ever on man's shoulders; and when the attempt is made to cast it off, it but returns upon us with more unfamiliar and more awful pressure. Second, because, as my narrative will make, alas! too evident, my discoveries were incomplete. Enough, then, that I not only recognised my natural body for the mere aura and effulgence of certain of the powers that made up my spirit, but managed to compound a drug by which these powers should be dethroned from their supremacy, and a second form and countenance substituted, none the less natural to me because they were the expression, and bore the stamp, of lower elements in my soul.

I hesitated long before I put this theory to the test of practice. I knew well that I risked death; for any drug that so potently controlled and shook the very fortress of identity, might by the least scruple of an overdose or at the least inopportunity in the moment of exhibition, utterly blot out that immaterial tabernacle which I looked to it to change. But the temptation of a discovery so singular and profound at last overcame the suggestions of alarm. I had long since prepared my tincture; I purchased at once, from a firm of wholesale chemists, a large quantity of a particular salt, which I knew, from my experiments, to be the last ingredient required; and, late one accursed night, I compounded the elements, watched them boil and smoke together in the glass, and when the ebullition had subsided, with a strong glow of courage, drank off the potion.

The most racking pangs succeeded: a grinding in the bones, deadly nausea, and a horror of the spirit that cannot be exceeded at the hour of birth or death. Then these agonies began swiftly to subside, and I came to myself as if out of a great sickness. There was something strange in my sensations, something indescribably new and, from its very novelty, incredibly sweet. I felt younger, lighter, happier in body; within I was conscious of a heady recklessness, a current of disordered sensual images running like a mill race in my fancy, a solution of the bonds of obligation, an unknown but not an innocent freedom of the soul. I knew myself, at the first breath of this new life, to be more wicked, tenfold more wicked, sold a slave to my original evil; and the thought, in that moment, braced and delighted me like wine. I stretched out my hands, exulting in the freshness of these sensations; and in the act, I was suddenly aware that I had lost in stature.

There was no mirror, at that date, in my room; that which stands beside me as I write was brought there later on, and for the very purpose of those transformations. The night, however, was far gone into the morning—the morning, black as it was, was nearly ripe for the conception of the day—the inmates of my house were locked in the most rigorous hours of slumber; and I determined, flushed as I was with hope and triumph, to venture in my new shape as far as to my bedroom. I crossed the yard, wherein the constellations looked down upon me, I could have thought, with wonder, the first creature of that sort that their unsleeping vigilance had yet disclosed to them; I stole through the corridors, a stranger in my own house; and coming to my room, I saw for the first time the appearance of Edward Hyde.

I must here speak by theory alone, saying not that which I know, but that which I suppose to be most probable. The evil side of my nature, to which I had now transferred the stamping efficacy, was less robust and less developed than the good which I had just deposed. Again, in the course of my life, which had been, after all, nine-tenths a life of effort, virtue and control, it had been much less exercised and much less exhausted. And hence, as I think, it came about that Edward Hyde was so much smaller, slighter, and younger than Henry Jekyll. Even as good shone upon the countenance of the one, evil was written broadly and plainly on the face of the other. Evil besides (which I must still believe to be the lethal side of man) had left on that body an imprint of deformity and decay. And yet when I looked upon that ugly idol in the glass, I was conscious of no repugnance, rather of a leap of welcome. This, too, was myself. It seemed natural and human. In my eyes it bore a livelier image of the spirit, it seemed more express and single, than the imperfect and divided countenance I had been hitherto accustomed to call mine. And in so far I was doubtless right. I have observed that when I wore the semblance of Edward Hyde, none could come near to me at first without a visible misgiving of the flesh. This, as I take it, was because all human beings, as we meet them, are commingled out of good and evil: and Edward Hyde, alone, in the ranks of mankind, was pure evil.

I lingered but a moment at the mirror: the second and conclusive experiment had yet to be attempted; it yet remained to be seen if I had lost my identity beyond redemption and must flee before daylight from a house that was no longer mine; and hurrying back to my cabinet, I once more prepared and drank the cup, once more suffered the pangs of dissolution, and came to myself once more with the character, the stature, and the face of Henry Jekyll.

That night I had come to the fatal cross roads. Had I approached my discovery in a more noble spirit, had I risked the experiment while under the empire of generous or pious aspirations, all must have been otherwise,

and from these agonies of death and birth I had come
forth an angel instead of a fiend. The drug had no dis-
criminating action; it was neither diabolical nor divine;
it but shook the doors of the prisonhouse of my disposition; and, like the captives of Philippi,² that which stood
within ran forth. At that time my virtue slumbered; my
evil, kept awake by ambition, was alert and swift to seize
the occasion; and the thing that was projected was Edward Hyde. Hence, although I had now two characters
as well as two appearances, one was wholly evil, and the
other was still the old Henry Jekyll, that incongruous
compound of whose reformation and improvement I
had already learned to despair. The movement was thus
wholly toward the worse.

Even at that time, I had not yet conquered my aver-
sion to the dryness of a life of study. I would still be
merrily disposed at times; and as my pleasures were (to
say the least) undignified, and I was not only well
known and highly considered, but growing towards the
elderly man, this incoherency of my life was daily growing more unwelcome. It was on this side that my new
power tempted me until I fell in slavery. I had but to
drink the cup, to doff at once the body of the noted professor, and to assume, like a thick cloak, that of Edward
Hyde. I smiled at the notion; it seemed to me at the
time to be humorous; and I made my preparations with
the most studious care. I took and furnished that house
in Soho to which Hyde was tracked by the police; and
engaged as housekeeper a creature whom I well knew
to be silent and unscrupulous. On the other side, I announced to my servants that a Mr. Hyde (whom I described) was to have full liberty and power about my
house in the square; and, to parry mishaps, I even

called and made myself a familiar object in my second character. I next drew up that will to which you so much objected; so that if anything befell me in the person of Dr. Jekyll, I could enter on that of Edward Hyde without pecuniary loss. And thus fortified, as I supposed, on every side, I began to profit by the strange immunities of my position.

Men have before hired bravos to transact their crimes, while their own person and reputation sat under shelter. I was the first that ever did so for his pleasures. I was the first that could thus plod in the public eye with a load of genial respectability, and in a moment, like a schoolboy, strip off these lendings and spring headlong into the sea of liberty.[3] But for me, in my impenetrable mantle, the safety was complete. Think of it—I did not even exist! Let me but escape into my laboratory door, give me but a second or two to mix and swallow the draught that I had always standing ready; and, whatever he had done, Edward Hyde would pass away like the stain of breath upon a mirror; and there in his stead, quietly at home, trimming the midnight lamp in his study, a man who could afford to laugh at suspicion, would be Henry Jekyll.

The pleasures which I made haste to seek in my disguise were, as I have said, undignified; I would scarce use a harder term. But in the hands of Edward Hyde they soon began to turn towards the monstrous. When I would come back from these excursions, I was often plunged into a kind of wonder at my vicarious depravity. This familiar that I called out of my own soul, and sent forth alone to do his good pleasure, was a being inherently malign and villainous; his every act and thought centred on self; drinking pleasure with bestial avidity from any degree of torture to another; relentless like a man of stone. Henry Jekyll stood at times aghast before the acts of Edward Hyde; but the situation was apart from ordinary laws, and insidiously relaxed the grasp of conscience. It was Hyde, after all, and Hyde alone, that was guilty. Jekyll was no worse; he woke again to his good qualities seemingly unimpaired; he would even make haste, where it was possible, to undo the evil done by Hyde. And thus his conscience slumbered.

Into the details of the infamy at which I thus connived (for even now I can scarce grant that I committed it) I have no design of entering. I mean but to point out the warnings and the successive steps with which my chastisement approached. I met with one accident which, as it brought on no consequence, I shall no more than mention. An act of cruelty to a child aroused against me the anger of a passerby, whom I recognised the other day in the person of your kinsman; the doctor and the child's family joined him; there were moments when I feared for my life; and at last, in order to pacify their too just resentment, Edward Hyde had to bring them to the door, and pay them in a cheque drawn in the name of Henry Jekyll. But this danger was easily eliminated from the future by opening an account at another bank in the name of Edward Hyde himself; and when, by sloping my own hand backwards, I had supplied my double with a signature, I thought I sat beyond the reach of fate.

Some two months before the murder of Sir Danvers, I had been out for one of my adventures, had returned at a late hour, and woke the next day in bed with somewhat odd sensations. It was in vain I looked about me; in vain I saw the decent furniture and tall proportions of my room in the square; in vain that I recognised the pattern of the bed curtains and the design of the mahogany frame; something still kept insisting that I was not where I was, that I had not wakened where I seemed to be, but in the little room in Soho where I was accustomed to sleep in the body of Edward Hyde. I smiled to myself, and, in my psychological way, began lazily to inquire into the elements of this illusion, occasionally, even as I did so, dropping back into a comfortable morning doze. I was still so engaged when, in one of my more wakeful moments, my eye fell upon my hand. Now, the hand of Henry Jekyll (as you have often remarked) was professional in shape and size; it was large, firm, white and comely. But the hand which I now saw, clearly enough in the yellow light of a mid-London morning, lying half shut on the bed-clothes, was lean, corded, knuckly, of a dusky pallor, and thickly shaded with a swart growth of hair. It was the hand of Edward Hyde.

I must have stared upon it for near half a minute, sunk as I was in the mere stupidity of wonder, before terror woke up in my breast as sudden and startling as the crash of cymbals; and bounding from my bed, I rushed to the mirror. At the sight that met my eyes, my blood was changed into something exquisitely thin and icy. Yes, I had gone to bed Henry Jekyll, I had awakened Edward Hyde. How was this to be explained? I asked myself; and then, with another bound of terror—how was it to be remedied? It was well on in the morning; the servants were up; all my drugs were in the cabinet—a long journey, down two pairs of stairs, through the back passage, across the open court and through the anatomical theatre, from where I was then standing horror-struck. It might indeed be possible to cover my face; but of what use was that, when I was unable to conceal the alteration in my stature? And then, with an overpowering sweetness of relief, it came back upon my mind that the servants were already used to the coming and going of my second self. I had soon dressed, as well as I was able, in clothes of my own size; had soon passed through the house, where Bradshaw stared and drew back at seeing Mr. Hyde at such an hour and in such a strange array; and ten minutes later, Dr. Jekyll had returned to his own shape and was sitting down, with a darkened brow, to make a feint of breakfasting.

Small indeed was my appetite. This inexplicable incident, this reversal of my previous experience, seemed, like the Babylonian finger on the wall,[4] to be spelling out the letters of my judgment; and I began to reflect more seriously than ever before on the issues and possibilities of my double existence. That part of me which I had the power of projecting had lately been much exercised and nourished; it had seemed to me of late as though the body of Edward Hyde had grown in stature, as though (when I wore that form) I were conscious of a more generous tide of blood; and I began to spy a danger that, if this were much prolonged, the balance of my nature might be permanently overthrown, the power of voluntary change be forfeited, and the character of Edward Hyde become irrevocably mine. The power of the drug had not been always equally displayed. Once, very early in my career, it had totally failed me; since then I had been obliged on more than one occasion to double, and once, with infinite risk of death, to treble the amount; and these rare uncertainties had cast hitherto the sole shadow on my contentment. Now, however, and in the light of that morning's accident, I was led to remark that whereas, in the beginning, the difficulty had been to throw off the body of Jekyll, it had of late gradually but decidedly transferred itself to the other side. All things therefore seemed to point to this: that I was slowly losing hold of my original and better self, and becoming slowly incorporated with my second and worse.

Between these two I now felt I had to choose. My two natures had memory in common, but all other faculties were most unequally shared between them. Jekyll (who was composite) now with the most sensitive apprehensions, now with a greedy gusto, projected and shared in the pleasures and adventures of Hyde; but Hyde was indifferent to Jekyll, or but remembered him as the mountain bandit remembers the cavern in which he conceals himself from pursuit. Jekyll had more than a father's interest; Hyde had more than a son's indifference. To cast in my lot with Jekyll was to die to those appetites which I had long secretly indulged and had of late begun to pamper. To cast it in with Hyde was to die to a thousand interests and aspirations, and to become, at a blow and for ever, despised and friendless. The bargain might appear unequal; but there was still another consideration in the scales; for while Jekyll would suffer smartingly in the fires of abstinence, Hyde would be not even conscious of all that he had lost. Strange as my circumstances were, the terms of this debate are as old and commonplace as man; much the same inducements and alarms cast the die for any tempted and trembling sinner; and it fell out with me, as it falls with so vast a majority of my fellows, that I chose the better part and was found wanting in the strength to keep to it.

Yes, I preferred the elderly and discontented doctor, surrounded by friends and cherishing honest hopes; and bade a resolute farewell to the liberty, the comparative youth, the light step, leaping pulses and secret pleasures, that I had enjoyed in the disguise of Hyde. I made this choice perhaps with some unconscious reservation, for I neither gave up the house in Soho, nor destroyed the clothes of Edward Hyde, which still lay ready in my cabinet. For two months, however, I was true to my determination; for two months I led a life of such severity as I had never before attained to, and enjoyed the compensations of an approving conscience. But time began at last to obliterate the freshness of my alarm; the praises of conscience began to grow into a thing of course; I began to be tortured with throes and longings, as of Hyde struggling after freedom; and at last, in an hour of moral weakness, I once again compounded and swallowed the transforming draught.

I do not suppose that when a drunkard reasons with himself upon his vice, he is once out of five hundred times affected by the dangers that he runs through his brutish physical insensibility; neither had I, long as I had considered my position, made enough allowance for the complete moral insensibility and insensate readiness to evil which were the leading characters of Edward Hyde. Yet it was by these that I was punished. My devil had been long caged, he came out roaring. I was conscious, even when I took the draught, of a more unbridled, a more furious propensity to ill. It must have been this, I suppose, that stirred in my soul that tempest of impatience with which I listened to the civilities of my unhappy victim; I declare at least, before God, no man morally sane could have been guilty of that crime upon so pitiful a provocation; and that I struck in no more reasonable spirit than that in which a sick child may break a plaything. But I had voluntarily stripped myself of all those balancing instincts by which even the worst of us continues to walk with some degree of steadiness among temptations; and in my case, to be tempted, however slightly, was to fall.

Instantly the spirit of hell awoke in me and raged. With a transport of glee, I mauled the unresisting body, tasting delight from every blow; and it was not till weariness had begun to succeed that I was suddenly, in the top fit of my delirium, struck through the heart by a cold thrill of terror. A mist dispersed; I saw my life to be forfeit; and fled from the scene of these excesses, at once glorying and trembling, my lust of evil gratified and stimulated, my love of life screwed to the topmost peg. I ran to the house in Soho, and (to make assurance doubly sure) destroyed my papers; thence I set out through the lamplit streets, in the same divided ecstasy of mind, gloating on my crime, light-headedly devising others in the future, and yet still hastening and still harkening in my wake for the steps of the avenger. Hyde had a song upon his lips as he compounded the draught, and as he drank it pledged the dead man. The pangs of transformation had not done tearing him, before Henry Jekyll, with streaming tears of gratitude and remorse, had fallen upon his knees and lifted his clasped hand to God. The veil of self-indulgence was rent from head to foot, I saw my life as a whole: I followed it up from the days of childhood, when I had walked with my father's hand, and through the self-denying toils of my professional life, to arrive again and again, with the same sense of unreality, at the damned horrors of the evening. I could have screamed aloud; I sought with tears and prayers to smother down the crowd of hideous images and sounds with which my memory swarmed against me; and still, between the petitions, the ugly face of my iniquity stared into my soul. As the acuteness of this remorse began to die away, it was succeeded by a sense of joy. The problem of my conduct was solved. Hyde was henceforth impossible; whether I would or not, I was now confined to the better part of my existence; and, oh, how I rejoiced to think it! with what willing humility I embraced anew the restrictions of natural life! with what sincere renunciation I locked the door by which I had so often gone and come, and ground the key under my heel!

The next day came the news that the murder had been overlooked, that the guilt of Hyde was patent to the world, and that the victim was a man high in public estimation. It was not only a crime, it had been a tragic folly. I think I was glad to know it; I think I was glad to have my better impulses thus buttressed and guarded by the terrors of the scaffold. Jekyll was now my city of refuge; let but Hyde peep out an instant, and the hands of all men would be raised to take and slay him.

I resolved in my future conduct to redeem the past; and I can say with honesty that my resolve was fruitful of some good. You know yourself how earnestly in the last months of last year I laboured to relieve suffering; you know that much was done for others, and that the days passed quietly, almost happily for myself. Nor can I truly say that I wearied of this beneficent and innocent life; I think instead that I daily enjoyed it more completely; but I was still cursed with my duality of purpose; and as the first edge of my penitence wore off, the lower side of me, so long indulged, so recently chained down, began to growl for licence. Not that I dreamed of resuscitating Hyde; the bare idea of that would startle me to frenzy: no, it was in my own person that I was once more tempted to trifle with my conscience; and it was as an ordinary secret sinner that I at last fell before the assaults of temptation.

There comes an end to all things; the most capacious measure is filled at last; and this brief condescension to my evil finally destroyed the balance of my soul. And yet I was not alarmed; the fall seemed natural, like a return to the old days before I had made my discovery. It was a fine, clear January day, wet under foot where the frost had melted, but cloudless overhead; and the Regent's Park was full of winter chirrupings and sweet with Spring odours. I sat in the sun on a bench; the animal within me licking the chops of memory; the spiritual side a little drowsed, promising subsequent penitence, but not yet moved to begin. After all, I reflected, I was like my neighbours; and then I smiled, comparing myself with other men, comparing my active goodwill with the lazy cruelty of their neglect. And at the very moment of that vainglorious thought, a qualm came over me, a horrid nausea and the most deadly shuddering. These passed away, and left me faint; and then as in its turn the faintness subsided, I began to be aware of a change in the temper of my thoughts, a greater boldness, a contempt of danger, a solution of the bonds of obligation. I looked down; my clothes hung formlessly on my shrunken limbs; the hand that lay on my knee was corded and hairy. I was once more Edward Hyde. A moment before I had been safe of all men's respect, wealthy, beloved—the cloth laying for me in the dining-room at home; and now I was the common quarry of mankind, hunted, houseless, a known murderer, thrall to the gallows.

My reason wavered, but it did not fail me utterly. I have more than once observed that, in my second character, my faculties seemed sharpened to a point and my spirits more tensely elastic; thus it came about that, where Jekyll perhaps might have succumbed, Hyde rose to the importance of the moment. My drugs were in one of the presses of my cabinet: how was I to reach them? That was the problem that (crushing my temples in my hands) I set myself to solve. The laboratory door I had closed. If I sought to enter by the house, my own servants would consign me to the gallows. I saw I must employ another hand, and thought of Lanyon. How was he to be reached? how persuaded? Supposing that I escaped capture in the streets, how was I to make my way into his presence? and how should I, an unknown and displeasing visitor, prevail on the famous physician to rifle the study of his colleague, Dr. Jekyll? Then I remembered that of my original character, one part remained to me: I could write my own hand; and once I had conceived that kindling spark, the way that I must follow became lighted up from end to end.

Thereupon, I arranged my clothes as best I could, and summoning a passing hansom, drove to an hotel in Portland Street, the name of which I chanced to remember. At my appearance (which was indeed comical enough, however tragic a fate these garments covered) the driver could not conceal his mirth. I gnashed my teeth upon him with a gust of devilish fury; and the smile withered from his face—happily for him—yet more happily for myself, for in another instant I had certainly dragged him from his perch. At the inn, as I entered, I looked about me with so black a countenance as made the attendants tremble; not a look did they exchange in my presence; but obsequiously took my orders, led me to a private room, and brought me wherewithal to write. Hyde in danger of his life was a creature new to me: shaken with inordinate anger, strung to the pitch of murder, lusting to inflict pain. Yet the creature was astute; mastered his fury with a great effort of the will; composed his two important letters, one to Lanyon and one to Poole, and, that he might receive actual evidence of their being posted, sent them out with directions that they should be registered.

Thenceforward, he sat all day over the fire in the private room, gnawing his nails; there he dined, sitting alone with his fears, the waiter visibly quailing before his eye; and thence, when the night was fully come, he set forth in the corner of a closed cab, and was driven to and fro about the streets of the city. He, I say—I cannot say, I. That child of Hell had nothing human; nothing lived in him but fear and hatred. And when at last, thinking the driver had begun to grow suspicious, he discharged the cab and ventured on foot, attired in his misfitting clothes, an object marked out for observation, into the midst of the nocturnal passengers, these two base passions raged within him like a tempest. He walked fast, hunted by his fears, chattering to himself, skulking through the less frequented thoroughfares, counting the minutes that still divided him from midnight. Once a woman spoke to him, offering, I think, a box of lights.[5] He smote her in the face, and she fled.

When I came to myself at Lanyon's, the horror of my old friend perhaps affected me somewhat: I do not

know; it was at least but a drop in the sea to the abhor-
rence with which I looked back upon these hours. A
change had come over me. It was no longer the fear of
the gallows, it was the horror of being Hyde that racked
me. I received Lanyon's condemnation partly in a
dream; it was partly in a dream that I came home to my
own house and got into bed. I slept after the prostration
of the day, with a stringent and profound slumber which
not even the nightmares that wrung me could avail to
break. I awoke in the morning shaken, weakened, but
refreshed. I still hated and feared the thought of the
brute that slept within me, and I had not of course forgotten the appalling dangers of the day before; but I
was once more at home, in my own house and close to
my drugs; and gratitude for my escape shone so strong
in my soul that it almost rivalled the brightness of hope.

I was stepping leisurely across the court after breakfast, drinking the chill of the air with pleasure, when I
was seized again with those indescribable sensations that
heralded the change; and I had but the time to gain the
shelter of my cabinet, before I was once again raging and
freezing with the passions of Hyde. It took on this occasion a double dose to recall me to myself; and alas, six
hours after, as I sat looking sadly in the fire, the pangs returned, and the drug had to be re-administered. In
short, from that day forth it seemed only by a great effort
as of gymnastics, and only under the immediate stimula-
tion of the drug, that I was able to wear the countenance
of Jekyll. At all hours of the day and night I would be
taken with the premonitory shudder; above all, if I slept,
or even dozed for a moment in my chair, it was always as
Hyde that I awakened. Under the strain of this continually impending doom and by the sleeplessness to which

I now condemned myself, ay, even beyond what I had thought possible to man, I became, in my own person, a creature eaten up and emptied by fever, languidly weak both in body and mind, and solely occupied by one thought: the horror of my other self. But when I slept, or when the virtue of the medicine wore off, I would leap almost without transition (for the pangs of transformation grew daily less marked) into the possession of a fancy brimming with images of terror, a soul boiling with causeless hatreds, and a body that seemed not strong enough to contain the raging energies of life. The powers of Hyde seemed to have grown with the sickliness of Jekyll. And certainly the hate that now divided them was equal on each side. With Jekyll, it was a thing of vital instinct. He had now seen the full deformity of that creature that shared with him some of the phenomena of consciousness, and was co-heir with him to death: and beyond these links of community, which in themselves made the most poignant part of his distress, he thought of Hyde, for all his energy of life, as of something not only hellish but inorganic. This was the shocking thing; that the slime of the pit seemed to utter cries and voices; that the amorphous dust gesticulated and sinned; that what was dead, and had no shape, should usurp the offices of life. And this again, that that insurgent horror was knit to him closer than a wife, closer than an eye; lay caged in his flesh, where he heard it mutter and felt it struggle to be born; and at every hour of weakness, and in the confidences of slumber, prevailed against him, and deposed him out of life. The hatred of Hyde for Jekyll was of a different order. His terror of the gallows drove him continually to commit temporary suicide, and return to his subordinate station of a part instead of a person; but he loathed the necessity, he loathed the despondency into which Jekyll was now fallen, and he resented the dislike with which he was himself regarded. Hence the ape-like tricks that he would play me, scrawling in my own hand blasphemies on the pages of my books, burning the letters and destroying the portrait of my father; and indeed, had it not been for his fear of death, he would long ago have ruined himself in order to involve me in the ruin. But his love of life is wonderful; I go further: I, who sicken and freeze at the mere thought of him, when I recall the abjection and passion of this attachment, and when I know how he fears my power to cut him off by suicide, I find it in my heart to pity him.

It is useless, and the time awfully fails me, to prolong this description; no one has ever suffered such torments, let that suffice; and yet even to these, habit brought—no, not alleviation—but a certain callousness of soul, a certain acquiescence of despair; and my punishment might have gone on for years, but for the last calamity which has now fallen, and which has finally severed me from my own face and nature. My provision of the salt, which had never been renewed since the date of the first experiment, began to run low. I sent out for a fresh supply, and mixed the draught; the ebullition followed, and the first change of colour, not the second; I drank it, and it was without efficiency. You will learn from Poole how I have had London ransacked; it was in vain; and I am now persuaded that my first supply was impure, and that it was that unknown impurity which lent efficacy to the draught.

About a week has passed, and I am now finishing this statement under the influence of the last of the old powders. This, then, is the last time, short of a miracle, that Henry Jekyll can think his own thoughts or see his own face (now how sadly altered!) in the glass. Nor must I delay too long to bring my writing to an end; for if my narrative has hitherto escaped destruction, it has been by a combination of great prudence and great good luck. Should the throes of change take me in the act of writing it, Hyde will tear it in pieces; but if some time shall have elapsed after I have laid it by, his wonderful selfishness and circumscription to the moment will probably save it once again from the action of his ape-like spite. And indeed the doom that is closing on us both has already changed and crushed him. Half an hour from now, when I shall again and for ever reindue that hated personality, I know how I shall sit shuddering and weeping in my chair, or continue, with the most strained and fearstruck ecstasy of listening, to pace up and down this room (my last earthly refuge) and give ear to every sound of menace. Will Hyde die upon the scaffold? or will he find the courage to release himself at the last moment? God knows; I am careless; this is my true hour of death, and what is to follow concerns another than myself. Here, then, as I lay down the pen, and proceed to seal up my confession, I bring the life of that unhappy Henry Jekyll to an end.

NOTES

Story of the Door

1. **Cain's heresy:** An allusion to the story of Cain's murder of Abel in Genesis 4 of the Bible. The heresy is Cain's retort to God's question, "Where is Abel thy brother?" to which he answers, "Am I my brother's keeper?" Utterson's paraphrase is deliberately cavalier and revisionary.
2. **distained:** Discolored.
3. **Juggernaut:** Any massive, inexorable force destroying everything in its path. The term comes from "Jaggannath," the Hindi title of the eighth avatar of the god Vishnu, literally "lord of the world" (*Jagga* for world; *natha* for protector). An idol of this deity was dragged annually in procession on an enormous chariot, under the wheels of which devotees are said to have thrown themselves to be crushed to death; reports of this ritual entered England in the late 1300s and persisted through the nineteenth century.

4. **gave a view halloa:** Shout given by hunter on seeing a fox.
5. **Sawbones:** Slang for doctor, especially a surgeon.
6. **struck:** Surrendered.
7. **Coutts's:** The most prestigious bank in Great Britain, serving the wealthy elite.
8. **pink of the proprieties:** The height of respectability.
9. **Queer Street:** Nineteenth-century London slang for the imaginary residence of those in financial difficulties or for any potentially scandalous circumstance. See also the American slang term "easy street." Charles Dickens used the term in *Our Mutual Friend* (1865): "Queer Street is full of lodgers just at present."

Search for Mr. Hyde

1. **M.D., D.C.L., LL.D., F.R.S.:** Dr. Jekyll's professional credentials: "Doctor of Medicine," "Doctor of Civil Law," "Doctor of Law," "Fellow of the Royal Society" (for scientists).
2. **Damon and Pythias:** In Greek legend, two men who became an emblem of loyal friendship. In the first half of the fourth century B.C., Damon and Pythias, Pythagoreans, visited Syracuse, where Pythias was arrested on trumped-up charges of spying and conspiracy against the tyrant Dionysius, who ordered his execution. Pythias was allowed to go home to settle his affairs, with Damon held in security for his return. When Pythias's return was delayed, Damon was led off for execution and was saved only by the last-minute arrival of Pythias.

Dionysius was so impressed by their mutual loyalty that he pardoned both of them.

3. **conveyancing:** The drawing of legal documents to transfer ownership.

4. **mere:** Absolute.

5. **where his friend lay . . . he must rise and do its bidding:** An evocation of the scene in Mary Shelley's *Frankenstein,* in which Victor Frankenstein describes his interrupted sleep the night after he creates the monster: "By the dim and yellow light of the moon, as it forced its way through the window-shutters, I beheld the wretch—the miserable monster whom I had created. He held up the curtain of the bed; and his eyes, if eyes they may be called, were fixed on me . . . one hand was stretched out, seemingly to detain me."

6. **troglodytic:** A term from the Greek *trogle* meaning "hole or cave" and *dyein* meaning "to enter," referring literally to primitive cave dwellers. Figuratively, the term means any person who is so socially uncouth, reclusive, or unworldly as to evoke this description.

7. **the old story of Dr. Fell:** Dr. John Fell (1625–1686) was an English doctor, prelate, and dean of Christ Church, Oxford University. Fell promised to cancel the expulsion of Thomas Brown (1663–1704) if Brown could provide an on-the-spot translation of Martial's thirty-third epigram: *Non amo te, Sabidi, nec possum dicere quare; / Hoc tantum possum non amo te,* which translates: "I do not love you, Sabidi, nor can I say why; / This much I can—I do not love you." Brown famously replied with the following: "I do not love thee, Dr. Fell, /

The reason why I cannot tell; / But this I know, and know full well, / I do not love thee, Dr. Fell."

8. **clay continent:** A metaphor for the human body.
9. **old Harry:** A term of affection here, it is also a slang term for the devil, a reference Utterson evokes when he describes Hyde in this same sentence as bearing "Satan's signature" on his face.
10. **Poole:** An allusion to Grace Poole, the keeper of Bertha Mason, Edward Rochester's mad wife, secretly lodged in the attic of Thornfield Hall in Charlotte Brontë's novel *Jane Eyre* (1847).
11. *pede claudo:* A Latin term meaning "on halting foot." In this context, the phrase refers to the way past sins slowly but inevitably catch up with a person.
12. **Jack-in-the-Box:** A child's toy, in which a puppet on a spring inside a box jumps out suddenly when the box is opened.

The Carew Murder Case

1. **gin palace:** A cheap drinking establishment.
2. **penny numbers:** Serialized popular stories, also called "penny dreadfuls."

Incident of the Letter

1. **theatre:** A surgical theater. Seats for student observers are arranged around a central surgical demonstration area.
2. **cheval-glass:** A long mirror that is set in a frame so that it can be tilted.
3. **M.P.:** An abbreviation for "Member of Parliament."

The Last Night

1. **wrack:** A layer of clouds.
2. **lawny:** Resembling the fabric lawn, which is light and fine.
3. **strong smell of kernels:** Cyanide, a powerful poison, smells like bitter almond kernels.

Dr. Lanyon's Narrative

1. *10th December 18—:* The letter should be dated the 9th of January, 18—, according to the opening sentence of this chapter and other time references in the story. The date on the letter is a mistake Stevenson made in his haste to write the book.
2. **bull's eye open:** With the sliding door of a lantern open.

Henry Jekyll's Full Statement of the Case

1. **perennial war among my members:** The conflict among parts of himself. The phrase alludes to James 4 of the Bible: "From whence come wars and fightings among you? Come they not hence, even of your lusts that war in your members?"
2. **Captives of Philippi:** According to Acts 16:26 of the Bible, the apostle Paul and his companion Silas were imprisoned in Philippi, when an earthquake shook the foundations of the prison, loosening the locks on the gates. Rather than fleeing, Paul and the other prisoners remained were they were, sparing the prison guard's sure punishment.

3. **strip off these lendings and spring headlong into the sea of liberty:** The phrase "strip off these lendings" is an allusion to William Shakespeare's play *King Lear.* Lear gives out a cry when the ragged beggar "poor Tom" enters his hovel on the heath. Struck by the sense that the beggar is "no more but such a poor, bare, forked animal," Lear tears off his own clothes, saying, "Off, off you lendings!" The liberty Lear experiences is a release from any illusions of his difference from Tom and an acknowledgment of their common lot.

4. **Babylonian finger on the wall:** A reference to the incident in the Bible (Daniel 5) in which King Belshazzar of Babylon sees a man's fingers writing a mysterious message on the wall of his palace. The prophet Daniel is called in to interpret the writing, and translates it as "You have been weighed in the balance and found wanting." He interprets the writing as a sign of God's future punishment of the king for his arrogance and defiance. The phrase "the writing is on the wall," meaning doom is foretold, comes from this Bible story.

5. **box of lights:** Matches.

INTERPRETIVE NOTES

The Plot

The Strange Case of Dr. Jekyll and Mr. Hyde opens with Richard Enfield telling lawyer Gabriel Utterson how he witnessed a mysterious and repellent figure named Mr. Hyde trample a young girl on a nighttime London street. Threatened by the crowd, Hyde agrees to pay the child's family reparations of one hundred pounds and retrieves a check from an old building. Although Enfield is reluctant to disclose the name on the check, his listener, lawyer Gabriel Utterson, reveals that he already knows it to be that of his client and friend, Dr. Henry Jekyll.

Jekyll has given Utterson a will designating Hyde as Jekyll's main beneficiary. Bothered by the will and Hyde's crime, Utterson becomes obsessed with seeing him. One evening, Utterson intercepts Hyde at the same old building he entered to get the check, which turns out to be the old laboratory entrance to Jekyll's home. Utterson speaks with Dr. Jekyll's butler, Poole, who says Hyde has a key to the laboratory door and that Dr. Jekyll has instructed the servants to obey Hyde. Convinced Hyde is blackmailing Jekyll, Utterson confronts Jekyll about Hyde. Jekyll refuses to discuss the situation, but extracts Utterson's promise that he will carry out the will benefiting Hyde.

A year later, the city is shocked by the brutal murder of Sir Danvers Carew. A maid tells the police she saw Hyde beating Carew to death with a walking cane and then fleeing the scene. The police find a letter addressed to Utterson on the victim, and alert him. Utterson affirms that the victim is his client, Carew, and, upon recognizing the broken half of the cane at the crime scene as Jekyll's, takes the inspector to Hyde's home. At Hyde's place, an unpleasant maid answers the door and says that Hyde has left early that evening. Going through the place, the inspector and Utterson find a half-burned checkbook and the other half of the walking stick. A check made out in thousands of pounds to Hyde confirms both men's suspicions.

The next afternoon, Utterson confronts Jekyll in his laboratory and asks if he is hiding Hyde. Looking shaken, Jekyll emphatically states that he is done with Hyde and that he will never see him again. Jekyll gives Utterson a letter from Hyde. In it, Hyde tells Jekyll not to worry about his safety as he has a plan of escape. Utterson takes the letter with him to his house, where his assistant, Mr. Guest, notes the handwriting is identical to Jekyll's except for the slant.

Hyde disappears, and for two months, Jekyll returns to his good old ways. Then, suddenly, Jekyll refuses to receive visitors. Vexed, Utterson visits Dr. Lanyon,

Jekyll's colleague. Lanyon, on the verge of death, says that he has had a terrible shock and refuses to discuss Jekyll. Utterson writes to Jekyll, who sends him a letter affirming that he has had a falling-out with Lanyon and stating that henceforth he will lead a life of "extreme seclusion." After Lanyon's death a few weeks later, Utterson opens a letter from Lanyon, which contains only another envelope marked "not to be opened till the death or disappearance of Dr. Henry Jekyll." Utterson places the letter in his safe. He attempts to visit Jekyll but is rebuffed, and Poole reports that Jekyll is confined to his laboratory. Later, Utterson and Enfield briefly spy a sickly Jekyll through a window.

Finally a distraught Poole appears at Utterson's and asks him to come to Jekyll's. Someone has been shut up in Jekyll's laboratory, asking for medicines, and Poole suspects Hyde has murdered Jekyll. Utterson and Poole break into the lab and discover Hyde's body. Searching for Jekyll, they find a chemical experiment, a blasphemed religious book, a looking glass, and an envelope addressed to Mr. Utterson. Inside are a revised will benefiting Utterson, a sealed letter, and a note from Jekyll telling Utterson to read the sealed document only after reading Lanyon's letter.

Lanyon's letter reveals that he had received a letter from Jekyll requesting him to have a locksmith open the door to his lab, bring a drawer of vials and powders back to his house, and let a visitor into his home on Jekyll's behalf. Lanyon fulfilled Jekyll's strange requests. After seizing the drawer and mixing a combination of its chemicals, the visitor warned Lanyon to go away while he drank the potion. Lanyon remained in the room and witnessed the transformation of the visitor into Jekyll.

Jekyll then confessed that the former being was indeed Hyde.

The last chapter relates the contents of Jekyll's final letter to Utterson. In it, Jekyll describes his motivations for separating out his good and evil natures, and the reckless scientific experiments that led to the birth of Mr. Hyde. He recounts how these experiments at first succeeded and then gradually went horribly awry, leading to the events of the past months and, eventually, the death of both Jekyll and Hyde.

The Characters

Dr. Henry Jekyll. A large, amiable man, the doctor is a well-liked member of a society of successful, professional bachelors. He values his excellent reputation and obeys the rules of Victorian society but longs for forbidden pleasure.

Edward Hyde. Jekyll's evil persona. Notably smaller, younger, and more energetic than Jekyll, Hyde displays a lust for life as he rampages and indulges in various undisclosed pleasures. Violent, hairy, and "ape-like," Hyde resents Jekyll's timid, repressed ways.

Gabriel John Utterson. Our primary narrator. A prominent attorney and close friend of Dr. Jekyll's, Utterson is the epitome of the professional Victorian bachelor. Utterson is solid and self-denying, but fascinated by Hyde. As Jekyll's trusted friend, Utterson receives all the important documents in the tale, including Jekyll's two wills, Lanyon's letter, and Hyde's final disclosure of the events.

Dr. Hastie Lanyon. A robust doctor with a firm belief in objective science. He and Jekyll were childhood friends but parted ways over Jekyll's scientific interests, which Lanyon found foolish and misguided. Jekyll, in turn, calls Lanyon a "hide-bound pedant."

Richard Enfield. Utterson's cousin and Sunday morning strolling companion. A rather staid character, Enfield is the first to remark on Hyde's horrifying appearance as he relates Hyde's trampling of the little girl.

Poole. The butler in Dr. Jekyll's house. He plays an instrumental role in the plot by reporting on the activities in the house and bringing Utterson to Jekyll's house.

Bradshaw. Another servant in Dr. Jekyll's abode.

Sir Danvers Carew. A well-known member of Parliament who is murdered by Hyde.

Inspector Newcomen. The inspector who investigates the murder of Sir Danvers Carew.

Symbols and Themes

Man's double being. The central theme of the novel is, as Stevenson puts it, "that strong sense of man's double being, which must at times come in upon and overwhelm the mind of every thinking creature." The desire to separate the good, rule-obeying, publicly respectable self from the evil, violent, sensual self is what drives Dr. Jekyll to his ill-fated experiments. Hyde embodies the youthful, physically strong, amoral, murderous, and indulgent side of humanity, which is kept in check and hidden by the upright, self-denying, public-minded Jekyll. It is important to remember that Jekyll recognizes that while Hyde is pure evil, Jekyll himself is not pure good. After the experiment, he remains what he was before: a complex mixture of good and bad, but with a public face that appears to be wholly respectable. Eventually, the more vigorous and ever more greedy and violent Hyde overtakes Jekyll, eventually ensuring both their deaths. What Jekyll discovers is that the two sides of humankind are, in fact, inseparable and that the attempt to disassociate the good from the bad is folly.

Repression and Victorian society. In *Jekyll and Hyde* Stevenson makes clear that Jekyll's desire to fight man's double being stems from the repressive strictures of late-Victorian society, and that it is the impossible Victorian standards of morality that themselves create hypocrisy and evil. Jekyll is motivated to create a separate evil self in order to indulge his sensual desires, which he cannot express as a prominent middle-aged member of society. Before the experiment goes awry, Jekyll enjoys the fact that he can enact his undisclosed pleasures in the guise of Hyde, without losing stature in the eyes of his peers and colleagues. Had Victorian society been less repressive, Jekyll might never have been interested in creating a separate self. In turn, Hyde's power stems from having been denied so long. Jekyll points out that Hyde is younger, smaller, and lighter than he is, because Jekyll has devoted his life to "effort, virtue, and control." When Jekyll temporarily resists becoming Hyde and then succumbs to drinking the potion, Hyde reemerges stronger than ever. It is the attempt to completely repress the sensual side—a key component of Victorian culture—that creates and feeds the monster.

Appearances, the hidden, the passage between. Appearances and reputations are vital to the characters in the novel. When Hyde tramples the little girl, Enfield and the policeman threaten to defame his name and thus ruin him. Fear of losing his public stature is what keeps Jekyll from doing the things he wants to do in the first place. Stevenson emphasizes the contrast between appearances and truth in objects as well as people. The gentlemen's houses are described as respectable and "handsome," while others are run-down, marked with graffiti, and bear "in every feature the marks of prolonged and sordid neglect." Sometimes these descriptions bear out, but more often they hide the reality behind the facade. The abundant puns in the novel emphasize this kind of doubleness as well. For example, the character named Hyde is both "the hidden" personified and the persona whom Jekyll hides behind. Jekyll's name is a pun as well (*je* means "I" in French, and "-kyll" = kill), as is Utterson's ("utter" = speak).

Along with the wordplay, Stevenson provides his characters with an abundance of passageways between the worlds of good and evil. Doorways and doors open up facades and let the characters penetrate within; wine and the more mysterious potions prepared in Jekyll's lab change the characters, or liberate them. While rich descriptions of light, including sunlight, lamplight, and firelight, are usually associated with clarity and getting to the truth, and darkness with evil and obscurity, the London fog, which appears especially whenever Hyde is around, provides a realistically mysterious setting in which the nature of people and things is unclear.

A society of bachelors. All of the major characters in *Jekyll and Hyde* are bachelors, who, contrary to Victorian norms, do not seek happiness in marriage or romantic union. They spend their evenings alone drinking wine or gin and engaging in quiet activities or in the company of each other. In other Victorian novels, female characters often serve as moral influences modulating the social world of the story. Stevenson deliberately bucked the trend of Victorian realism by writing the novel without a love interest. The relative solitude of each of the characters, including Jekyll, also enables Jekyll's transformation into Hyde, as he lives and works alone in his laboratory without the interference or help of others.

Multiple perspectives and documentation. Stevenson presents four distinct perspectives on the story: Utterson's fascination with the whole situation, Enfield's reluctance to pursue the mysteries further, Lanyon's dismissal and horror, and Jekyll's own confession. By creating multiple viewpoints, Stevenson emphasizes that every tale and every situation has more than one version and that no single version is necessarily the truth. His use of multiple perspectives also reinforces the theme of double or multiple beings and of hidden stories within stories. Like other novels of the era that concern issues of identity, *Dr. Jekyll and Mr. Hyde* also uses many forms of documentation to convey the story. The novel concludes with two letters—Lanyon's and Jekyll's—which offer competing and overlapping versions of the events. The reader is left to piece together the story and draw conclusions from these different texts.

CRITICAL EXCERPTS

Biographical Studies

Balfour, Graham. *The Life of Robert Louis Stevenson.*
New York: Charles Scribner's Sons, 1901.

Balfour, Stevenson's cousin and first biographer,
draws on conversations, Stevenson's letters, and his
other writings to relate the details of the author's life in
this two-volume biography.

For a period of nearly eight months he had been
unable to earn any money or to carry any work to a
conclusion, and it was therefore with the greatest
delight that in the beginning of May he received an
offer from Messrs. Cassell for the book-rights of
Treasure Island. "How much do you suppose? I
believe it would be an excellent jest to keep the
answer till my next letter. For two cents I would do
so. Shall I? Anyway I'll turn the page first. No—well,
a hundred pounds, all alive, O! A hundred jingling,

tingling, golden, minted quid. Is not this wonderful? . . . It is dreadful to be a great, big man, and not to be able to buy bread."

Calder, Jenni. *Robert Louis Stevenson: A Life Study.* New York: Oxford University Press, 1980.

In this literary biography, Calder describes how events in Stevenson's life influenced the development of his works.

"Markheim" came out just before *Jekyll and Hyde;* the dreaming of the latter clearly reflected current preoccupations. Louis's own uneasiness as resident of Skerryvore may have drawn to the surface again his preoccupation with the double life. "Markheim" concerns the committing of a bloody and pointless murder by a man who is possessed overpoweringly by the need to kill. It is a brief, intense little story with a cathartic quality, drawn out by the murderer's relief when he is able to admit his crime and give himself into the sheltering power of the Devil. It is the acknowledgment that evil has won, and that giving oneself up to it is comforting. The theme is enlarged in *Jekyll and Hyde,* the theme that Louis spoke of, in a subsequent letter to J. A. Symonds, as "that damned old business of the war in the members." It is the Calvinist view that man must maintain a constant struggle with evil, that the slightest lapse in vigilance will allow the Devil to triumph. The reality of evil, its ambivalence, its attractions, had always possessed Louis. The ambivalent characterization of Long John Silver, so easily the most attractive character in *Treasure Island,* reflects this. Louis's impatience with his father's anguished guilt, his condemnation of Calvinist negativism, and his absorption of the devil-ridden folklore of Scotland were all operating in *Jekyll and Hyde*.

Daiches, David. *Robert Louis Stevenson and His World.* London: Thames and Hudson, 1973.

Replete with photographs and portraits of Stevenson and his family, this biography elegantly recounts Stevenson's life from his Calvinist Scottish roots through his worldwide travels and death in Samoa.

Stevenson thus grew up in Georgian Edinburgh, amid elegant streets inhabited by genteel profession-al families. To the north, the city sloped down to the Firth of Forth, with the hills of Fife clearly visible, when not obscured by rain or sea fog, from the cor-ner of Heriot Row and Howe Street, only a few paces from the Stevenson house. To the south, across Queen Street Gardens and the symmetrically planned parallel thoroughfares of Queen Street, George Street and Princes Street, lay Princes Street Gardens, dominated by the Castle which guarded the picturesque and slum-filled Old Town. At the east end of Princes Street, where the North Bridge joined the Old Town with the New, lay Waverley Station, and the young Stevenson would watch from the bridge as the trains puffed out, yearning to join the travellers in adventuring to strange new places. Further east lay Holyrood and the lion shape of Arthur's Seat. To the west lay the little old Dean Village, unspoilt in its hollow by the Water of Leith. One could follow this stream to the north-west suburb of Colinton, where the boy's grandfather was minister, and there one was within a stone's throw of the Pentland Hills, which early laid a hold on his imagination. City elegance, city adventure, city squalor, but also streams and hills and lochs, and the sea never far away. Stevenson, who was to grow up to become above all things a novelist of *place*, fitting action to local atmosphere with a remarkable sense of topographical appropriateness, savoured as a boy all these aspects of his native city, and they remained always in his imagination.

Early Reviews and Interpretations

Hopkins, Gerard Manley. "Letter to Robert Bridges, October 28, 1886." *Gerard Manley Hopkins: Selected Letters.* Ed. Catherine Phillips. Oxford: Clarendon, 1990, 243–244.

In this letter to his friend and fellow poet, Hopkins disagrees with Bridges's criticisms of the novel and expresses his admiration for Stevenson's characterizations.

"Jekyll and Hyde" I have read. You speak of the "gross absurdity" of the interchange. Enough that it is impossible and might perhaps have been a little better masked: it must be connived at, and it gives rise to a fine situation. It is not more impossible than fairies, giants, heathen gods, and lots of things that literature teems with—and none more than yours. You are certainly wrong about Hyde being over-drawn: my Hyde is worse. The trampling scene is perhaps a convention: he [Stevenson] was thinking of something unsuitable for fiction. I can by no means grant that the characters are not characterised, though how deep the springs of their surface action are I am not yet clear. But the superficial touches of character are admirable: how can you be so blind as not to see them? e.g. Utterson frowning, biting the end of his finger, and saying to the butler "This strange tale you tell me, my man, a very strange tale." And Dr. Lanyon: "I used to like it, sir [life]; yes, sir, I liked it. Sometimes I think if we knew all" etc. These are worthy of Shakespeare.

James, Henry. *Century Magazine* (April 1888): 877–878.
In an assessment of Stevenson's writings, fellow novelist James expresses admiration for *Jekyll and Hyde's* brevity and vivid presentation.

Is *Dr. Jekyll and Mr. Hyde* a work of high philosophic intention, or simply the most ingenious and irresponsible of fictions? It has the stamp of a really imaginative production, that we may take it in different ways; but I suppose it would generally be called the most serious of the author's tales. It deals with the relation of the baser parts of man to his nobler, or the capacity for evil that exists in the most generous natures; and it expresses these things in a fable which is a wonderfully happy invention. The subject is endlessly interesting, and rich in all sorts of provocation, and Mr. Stevenson is to be congratulated on having touched the core of it. I may do him injustice, but it is, however, here, not the profundity of the idea which strikes me so much as the art of the presentation—the extremely successful form. There is a genuine feeling for the perpetual moral question, a fresh

sense of the difficulty of being good and the brutish-
ness of being bad; but what there is above all is a singular ability in holding the interest. I confess that
that, to my sense, is the most edifying thing in the
short, rapid, concentrated story, which is really a
masterpiece of concision.

Lang, Andrew. *The Saturday Review* 9 (Jan. 1886):
55–56.
Lang praises Stevenson's skill and originality in por-
traying the struggle between parts of the self.

Mr. Stevenson's idea, his secret (but a very open
secret) is that of the double personality in every man.
The mere conception is familiar enough. Poe used it
in *William Wilson,* and Gautier in *Le Chevalier
Double.* Yet Mr. Stevenson's originality of treatment
remains none the less striking and astonishing. The
double personality does not in his romance take the
form of a personified conscience, the *doppel ganger*
of the sinner, a "double" like his own double which
Goethe is fabled to have seen: No; the "separable
self" in this "strange case" is all unlike that in *William
Wilson,* and, with its unlikeness to its master, with its
hideous caprices, and appalling vitality, and terrible
power of growth and increase, is, to our thinking, a
notion as novel as it is terrific. We would welcome a
spectre, a ghoul, or even a vampire gladly, rather
than meet Mr. Edward Hyde.

Noble, James Ashcroft. *The Academy* 23 (Jan. 1886): 55.
Noble lauds the novel, stating that the book sur-
passes its packaging as an inexpensive "shilling story."

"The Strange Case of Dr. Jekyll and Mr. Hyde" is not an orthodox three-volume novel; it is not even a one-volume novel of the ordinary type; it is simply a paper-covered shilling story, belonging, so far as external appearance goes, to a class of literature familiarity with which has bred in the minds of most readers a certain measure of contempt. Appearances, it has been once or twice remarked, are deceitful; and in this case they are very deceitful indeed, for, in spite of the paper cover and the popular price, Mr. Stevenson's story distances so unmistakably its three-volume and one-volume competitors, that its only fitting place is the place of honour. It is, indeed, many years since English fiction has been enriched by any work at once so weirdly imaginative in conception and so faultlessly ingenious in construction as this little tale, which can be read with ease in a couple of hours.

The Times (of London) 25 Jan. 1886.
This anonymous review favorably compares the novel with the work of Edgar Allan Poe and places it in company with other contemporary novels such as George Eliot's *Romola*.

Naturally, we compare it with the sombre masterpieces of Poe, and we may say at once that Mr. Stevenson has gone far deeper. Poe embroidered richly in the gloomy grandeur of his imagination upon themes that were but too material, and not very novel—on the sinister destiny overshadowing a doomed family, on a living and breathing man kept prisoner in a coffin or vault, on the wild whirling of a human waif in the boiling eddies of the Maelstrom—

while Mr. Stevenson evolves the ideas of his story from the world that is unseen, enveloping everything in weird mystery, till at last it pleases him to give us the password. We are not going to tell his strange story, though we might well do so, and only excite the curiosity of our readers. We shall only say that we are shown the shrewdest of lawyers hopelessly puzzled by the inexplicable conduct of a familiar friend.

Wedgwood, Julia. *The Contemporary Review* (April 1886): 594–595.

Wedgwood praises Stevenson's powerful and compressed rendering of dilemmas of the self.

Whereas most fiction deals with the relation between man and woman (and the very fact that its scope is so much narrowed is a sign of the atomic character of our modern thought), the author of this strange tale takes an even narrower range, and sets himself to investigate the meaning of the word *self.* No woman's name occurs in the book, no romance is even suggested in it; it depends on the interest of an idea; but so powerfully is this interest worked out that the reader feels that the same material might have been spun out to cover double the space, and still have struck him as condensed and close-knit workmanship. It is one of those rare fictions which make one understand the value of temperance in art.

Critical Interpretations: 1900s to 1940s

Chesterton, G. K. *Robert Louis Stevenson.* New York: Dodd, Mead, 1928.

In this book, Chesterton reviews Stevenson's books in light of his life. In the section on *Dr. Jekyll and Mr. Hyde*, Chesterton defends Stevenson's novel against post-Victorian critics who dismissed the work as "cheap and obvious."

The real stab of the story is not in the discovery that the one man is two men; but in the discovery that the two men are one man. After all the diverse wandering and warring of those two incompatible beings, there was still only one man born and only one man buried. . . . The point of the story is not that a man *can* cut himself off from his conscience, but that he cannot. The surgical operation is fatal in the story. It is an amputation of which both the parts die. Jekyll, even in dying, declares the conclusion of the matter; that the load of man's moral struggle cannot be thus escaped. The reason is that there can never be equality between the evil and the good. Jekyll and Hyde are not twin brothers. They are rather, as one of them truly remarks, like father and son. After all, Jekyll created Hyde; Hyde would never have created Jekyll; he only destroyed Jekyll.

Daiches, David. *Robert Louis Stevenson*. Norfolk, Conn.: New Directions, 1947.
Daiches draws on biographical facts to support his critical interpretations of Stevenson's works in this important study.

Stevenson made a distinction between the romantic and the dramatic. "Drama is the poetry of conduct, romance the poetry of circumstance," he wrote. In his romantic novels, therefore, the "probability" does not lie in the relation between character and event but in the relation between incidents and setting. Character drawing in the romantic novel is therefore to be done in large, broad strokes, with none of the psychological delicacy demanded of the dramatic novel. There is no inevitability in the decisions taken by the characters, and no moral implication. Even Dr. Jekyll is not shown as taking his fateful decision to experiment in disassociation as a result of any characteristic weakness of character: his motives are indicated with the utmost brevity; the interest lies in the action only, and not in his relation to character. *Dr. Jekyll and Mr. Hyde* is not, however, a typical Stevensonian story at all, for it has not that close linking of incident to environment that characterises "The Merry Men" and "The Pavilion on the Links."

Critical Interpretations: 1950s and 1960s

Eigner, Edwin M. *Robert Louis Stevenson and Romantic Tradition.* Princeton: Princeton University Press: 1966.
  Eigner examines Stevenson's works in the context of the nineteenth-century prose romance tradition.

Jekyll was wrong in attempting to segregate the two sides of his life, and he was even more wrong in glorifying the one side while alternately condemning and indulging the other. His chemical experiment is simply a logical extension of this treatment. It is by no means a new departure. The Spencer Tracy movie . . . makes a great deal of Jekyll's noble attempt to eradicate the evil in man's nature, but Stevenson's Jekyll is at least as much interested in freeing his evil nature from restraint as he is in giving scope to the good in him. . . . According to Jekyll . . . each of the two natures is dear to him, and he sees himself as "radically both."

Miyoshi, Masao. *The Divided Self: A Perspective on the Literature of the Victorians.* New York: New York University Press, 1969.

In the section on *Dr. Jekyll and Mr. Hyde,* Miyoshi discusses how the novel reflects the joylessness and repressed emotions and sexuality of Victorian life.

The important men of the book, then, are all unmarried, intellectually barren, emotionally stifled, joyless. Nor are things much different in the city as a whole. The more prosperous business people fix up their homes and shops, but in a fashion without chic. Houses give an appearance of "coquetry," and store fronts invite one like "rows of smiling saleswomen" (Chapter 1). The rather handsome town houses in the back streets of Dr. Jekyll's neighborhood are rented out to all sorts—"map-engravers, architects, shady lawyers, and the agents of obscure enterprises" (Chapter 2). Everywhere the fog of the dismal city is inescapable, even creeping under the doors and through the window jambs (Chapter 5). The setting hides a wasteland behind that secure and relatively comfortable respectability of its inhabitants. . . .

For the mastery of the book is the vision it conjures of the late Victorian wasteland, truly a de-Hyde-rated land unfit to sustain a human being simultaneously in an honorable public life and a joyful private one.

Nabokov, Vladimir. *Lectures on Literature*. Ed. Fredson Bowers. New York: Harcourt Brace Jovanovich, 1980.

In his lectures on "Masters of European Literature" given at Cornell University in the 1950s, novelist Nabokov expresses esteem for Stevenson's style in the writing of the novel.

There is a delightful winey taste about this book; in fact, a good deal of old mellow wine is drunk in the story: one recalls the wine that Utterson so comfortably sips. This sparkling and comforting draft is very different from the icy pangs caused by the chameleon liquor, the magic reagent that Jekyll brews in his dusty laboratory. Everything is very appetizingly put. Gabriel John Utterson of Gaunt Street mouths his words most roundly; there is an appetizing tang about the chill morning in London, and there is even a certain richness of tone in the description of the horrible sensations Jekyll undergoes during his *hydizations*. Stevenson had to rely on style very much in order to perform the trick, in order to master the two main difficulties confronting him: (1) to make the magic potion a plausible drug based on a chemist's ingredients and (2) to make Jekyll's evil side before and after the hydization a believable evil.

Critical Interpretations: 1970s and 1980s

Saposnik, Irving S. *Robert Louis Stevenson*. New York: Twayne, 1974.

This critical study of all of Stevenson's writings in-

cludes a chapter on the novel called "The Anatomy of
Dr. Jekyll and Mr. Hyde."

Hyde's literal power ends with his suicide, but his
metaphorical power is seemingly infinite. Many
things to his contemporaries, he has grown beyond
Stevenson's story in an age of automatic Freudian
response. As Hyde has grown, Jekyll has been over-
shadowed so that his role has shifted from culprit to
victim. Accordingly, the original fable has assumed a
meaning neither significant for the nineteenth century nor substantial for the twentieth. The time has
come for Jekyll and Hyde to be put back together
again.

Garrett, Peter K. "Cries and Voices: Reading *Jekyll and
Hyde.*" *Dr. Jekyll and Mr. Hyde after One Hundred
Years.* Ed. William Veeder and Gordon Hirsch.
Chicago: University of Chicago Press, 1988. 59–72.

In this essay, Garrett elucidates the instabilities of
meaning, narrative voices, and morality in Stevenson's
novel.

To consider whether any conception of *Jekyll and
Hyde*'s moral purpose can contain and stabilize its
tensions is to return to our initial question. The possibilities of reading we have been exploring suggest
that the tale's greatest power and interest derive less
from any high philosophic intention we may ascribe
to it than from its fictional irresponsibility, its refusal
or failure to offer any secure position for its reader or
to establish any fixed relation between its voices. The
conservative, ordering force of its moral oppositions

and the constraining coherence of its mystery plot lose their grip on a reading that recognizes the insidious, subversive effects we have traced. We may wonder, however, whether such a reading necessarily loses its own grip on the most obvious and fundamental features of the tale, the elements preserved by the perpetuation of its story as popular myth and its title as byword. A certain estrangement from the obvious and the popular does indeed seem necessary; stage, film, and television versions, as well as commonplace allusions (all the available ways of "knowing" *Jekyll and Hyde* without reading it), tend not only to reproduce but to exaggerate its dualism by making its moral oppositions more symmetrical. To undermine those oppositions is to challenge the common understanding of the tale.

Veeder, William. "Children of the Night: Stevenson and Patriarch." *Dr. Jekyll and Mr. Hyde after One Hundred Years.* Ed. William Veeder and Gordon Hirsch. Chicago: University of Chicago Press, 1988. 107–160.

In his essay, Veeder examines the representation of patriarchy in *Dr. Jekyll and Mr. Hyde.*

At stake in *Jekyll and Hyde* is nothing less than patriarchy itself, the social organization whose ideals and customs, transmissions of property and title, and locations of power privilege the male. Understanding the Fathers in *Jekyll and Hyde* is helped by seeing patriarchy both traditionally and locally: first in terms of its age-old obligations, then in terms of its immediate configuration in late-Victorian Britain. Traditionally the obligations of patriarchs are three:

to maintain the distinctions (master-servant, proper-improper) that ground patriarchy; to sustain the male ties (father-son, brother-brother) that constitute it; and to enter the wedlock (foregoing homosexuality) that perpetuates it. Exclusion and inclusion are the operative principles. Men must distinguish the patriarchal self from enemies, pretenders, competitors, corruptors; and they must affiliate through proper bonds at appropriate times. What Stevenson devastatingly demonstrates is that patriarchy behaves exactly counter to its obligations.

Critical Interpretations: 1990s through the Present

Brantlinger, Patrick. *The Reading Lesson: The Threat of Mass Literacy in Nineteenth-Century British Fiction*. Bloomington: Indiana University Press, 1998.

In his essay about *Dr. Jekyll and Mr. Hyde*, Brantlinger analyzes the novel as an allegory about the commercialization of literature and the rise of mass consumer society in the late-Victorian period.

When Utterson and Inspector Newcomen enter Hyde's Soho residence, they discover something quite different from its "blackguardly surroundings." The rooms Hyde uses are "furnished with luxury and good taste." They are evidently the rooms of an epicure who takes pleasure in art. "A closet was filled with wine; the plate was silver, the napery elegant; a good picture hung upon the walls, a gift (as Utterson supposed) from Henry Jekyll, who was much of a connoisseur; and the carpets were of many piles and agreeable in colour." Stevenson seems almost to be illustrating Oscar Wilde's thesis, in "Pen, Pencil, and Poison," that "there is no essential incongruity between crime and culture." Perhaps Hyde retains more of Jekyll's traits than just his handwriting. Or is the evidence of epicureanism pure Hyde, whereas Jekyll, like Utterson, adheres to a routine of abstinence and "dry divinity"? Whatever the case, the Soho flat is not some Fagin's roost in the underworld slums, but a setting that implies sensual enjoyment, perhaps libertinism, of an apparently upper-class sort. Further, there is more evidence of Hyde's reading in the apartment—unless it is Jekyll's reading—or perhaps it is evidence of his/his writing. The rooms, says Utterson, appeared to have been "recently and hurriedly ransacked," while on "the hearth there lay a pile of grey ashes, as though many papers had been burned."

Halberstam, Judith. *Skin Shows: Gothic Horror and the Technology of Monsters.* Durham and London: Duke University Press, 1995.

In the introduction to her critical study of Gothic literature, Halberstam analyzes the character of Jekyll/Hyde as an example of Gothic monstrosity—a hybrid of race, class, gender, and sexuality that is open to multiple interpretations.

In *Dracula* Bram Stoker directly copies Collins's style. Stevenson also uses Collins's narrative technique in *Dr. Jekyll and Mr. Hyde* but he frames his story in a more overtly legal setting so that our main narrator is a lawyer, the central document is the last will and testament of Dr. Jekyll, and all other accounts contribute to the "strange case." All Gothic novels employing this narrative device share an almost obsessive concern with documentation and they all exhibit a sinister mistrust of the not-said, the unspoken, the hidden, and the silent. Furthermore, most Gothic novels lack the point of view of the monster.

Linehan, Katherine Bailey. " 'Closer Than a Wife': The Strange Case of Dr. Jekyll's Significant Other." *Robert Louis Stevenson Reconsidered: New Critical Perspectives.* Ed. William B. Jones, Jr. Jefferson, N.C., and London: McFarland & Co., 2003.

Linehan examines the themes of repressed sexuality and divisions of the self in the novel in light of Stevenson's essays in "Lay Morals" and a letter he wrote to an American journalist, John Paul Bocock, in 1887.

To make a connection, finally, between the role of the diabolic in Jekyll and the absence of women at the center of the tale, we need to go back for a moment to the moral vision implied in Stevenson's letter to Bocock. Consider in particular the statement, "There is no harm in a voluptuary . . . malice and selfishness and cowardice . . . are the diabolic in man—not this poor wish to have a woman, that they make such a cry about." For Stevenson, the "war in the members"—a biblical phrase that Jekyll uses in the story—is not defined puritanically as a battle between virtuously celibate spirituality and wickedly fleshly sexuality. Instead, it involves a struggle to channel healthy, blameless physical appetites towards spiritually generous ends, so as to remain true to what one recognizes as one's best self. The danger lies in life's many temptations to compromise that best self by narrowly serving only a mean sort of self-gratification. Stumbles along the way are inevitable, so a degree of humility is indispensable to honest acknowledgment of mistakes made and of new efforts needed.

Oates, Joyce Carol. Foreword to *The Strange Case of Dr. Jekyll and Mr. Hyde.* New York: University of Nebraska Press, 1990.

In her foreword to this edition of the novel, Oates discusses how Stevenson anticipates Freudian theories of humankind's nature and dilemmas.

The visionary starkness of *The Strange Case of Dr. Jekyll and Mr. Hyde* anticipates that of Freud in such late melancholy meditations as *Civilization and Its Discontents* (1929–30): there is a split in man's psyche between ego and instinct, between civilization and "nature," and the split can never be healed. Freud saw ethics as a reluctant concession of the individual to the group, veneer of a sort overlaid upon an unregenerate primordial self. The various stratagems of culture—including, not incidentally, the "sublimation" of raw aggression by way of art and science—are ultimately powerless to contain the discontent, which must erupt at certain periodic times, on a collective scale, as war. Stevenson's quintessentially Victorian parable is unique in that the protagonist initiates his tragedy of doubleness out of a fully lucid sensibility—one might say a scientific sensibility. Dr. Jekyll knows what he is doing, and why he is doing it, though he cannot, of course, know how it will turn out. What is unquestioned throughout the narrative, by either Jekyll or his circle of friends, is mankind's fallen nature: sin is *original,* and *irremediable.* For Hyde, though hidden, will not remain so. And when Jekyll finally destroys him he must destroy Jekyll too.

Sandison, Alan. *"Jekyll and Hyde:* The Story of the Door." *Robert Louis Stevenson and the Appearance of Modernism.* New York: St. Martin's Press, 1996.

In this essay, Sandison analyzes the significance and symbolism of the door in *Jekyll and Hyde.*

In *Strange Case of Dr. Jekyll and Mr. Hyde,* the first chapter is given the title "Story of the Door" and so also raises certain expectations: principally, that we shall be given access to what lies behind it. The deferral of the fulfillment of these expectations not only heightens our interest and desire to know, it also gradually focuses more and more interest on the story as story, the text as text. When, in the penultimate chapter, an inner door—this door's double so to speak, a "red baize door" giving public access to the same space—is broken down by force, it discloses only the mute corpse of Edward Hyde; and another story, sealed in an enclosure. The owner of the "place with the door," as it is several times called, and the author of the story has vanished. But he has left more than a rack behind; he has left a text. By cunningly allowing for all this, Stevenson has opened another door and it is one which leads straight into the twentieth century.

Showalter, Elaine. *Sexual Anarchy: Gender and Culture at the Fin de Siècle.* New York: Viking, 1990.

In the chapter "Dr. Jekyll's Closet," Showalter analyzes the novel as a study of male hysteria and as a fable of repressed selves and desires.

> In the multiplication of narrative viewpoints that makes up the story, however, one voice is missing: that of Hyde himself. We never hear his account of the events, his memories of his strange birth, his pleasure and fear. Hyde's story would disturb the sexual economy of the text, the sense of panic at having liberated an uncontrollable desire. Hyde's hysterical narrative comes to us in two ways: in the representation of his feminine behavior, and in the body language of hysterical discourse. . . . Hyde's reality breaks through Jekyll's body in the shape of his hand, the timbre of his voice, and the quality of his gait.

QUESTIONS FOR DISCUSSION

The story of Dr. Jekyll's transformation is related mostly through Mr. Utterson's point of view. How does telling the story from a lawyer's point of view help Stevenson depict the world Jekyll inhabits?

Can you think of a person—in real life or in fiction or film—who leads a double life? What might motivate a person to create two (or more) distinct personas for himself or herself? Do you feel sometimes that you are two different people? How do you handle that feeling?

Many critics have written about the lack of female characters in the novel, proposing theories about why Stevenson may have left women out of the story. Why do you think Stevenson depicted mostly male characters? What female characters would you add to the story?

What were your reactions to Dr. Jekyll's final disclosure? Are his actions justified by his remorse and confessions of guilt? Do you think he deserves to have died or could there have been another remedy to the situation?

Who do you consider to be the most sympathetic character in the novel? Why? Are there any heroes in the story or are all the characters too flawed to be considered heroic?

The phrase "Dr. Jekyll and Mr. Hyde" is commonly used to describe a person with dramatically different sides to his or her personality. How accurate do you find this phrase in the context of the novel?

Since *Dr. Jekyll and Mr. Hyde* was published, many advances in genetics have been made, including the cloning of mammals and interspecies genetic modification of foods. What are your opinions on the proliferation of these practices? Can you envision a time in which Dr. Jekyll's remarkable transformation can really happen?

Stevenson's story has been retold many times, in children's books and in numerous plays and film productions. Why do you think this story is so appealing to so many people? If you were to retell the story in contemporary terms, how would you depict the character of Hyde?

SUGGESTIONS FOR THE INTERESTED READER

The Professor and the Madman: A Tale of Murder, Insanity, and the Making of the Oxford English Dictionary, by Simon Winchester. This is the true story story of two men who shaped the making of the *Oxford English Dictionary.* Winchester traces the interactions of the project's editor, Professor James Murray, and Dr. William Chester Minor, a voluminous contributor of entries and an American surgeon incarcerated for murder in Broadmoor—England's toughest institution for the criminally insane.

Mary Reilly, (VHS, DVD). Directed by Stephen Frears and based on Valerie Martin's 1990 novel of the same title, *Mary Reilly* (1996) tells the story of Jekyll and Hyde from the point of view of a maid in Dr. Jekyll's house. The title role is played by Julia Roberts, with John Malkovich as Dr. Jekyll.

Dr. Jekyll and Mr. Hyde (VHS, DVD). This lush black-and-white 1941 film production by director Victor Fleming is a classic in its own right. It considerably amends the plot of Stevenson's novel but retains all the complexity of its central themes. Spencer Tracy gives one of his most compelling performances as the mad doctor. Lana Turner plays a good girl with desires of her own to whom Tracy is engaged, while Ingrid Bergman plays a good-hearted bad girl he tortures as Mr. Hyde.

Sibyl, by Flora Rheta Schreiber. This classic 1973 story of one of the first diagnosed cases of multiple personality disorder tells the gripping story of Sybil Dorsett, a survivor of child abuse who was eventually diagnosed with sixteen separate personalities. In 1976, the book was turned into a made-for-television movie starring Sally Field.

FROM SIMON & SCHUSTER

SIMON & SCHUSTER PAPERBACKS
A CBS COMPANY